HIS BEAST RETURNS

EVERNIGHT PUBLISHING ®

www.evernightpublishing.com

ERIN M. LEAF

Copyright© 2019

Erin M. Leaf

Editor: Karyn White

Cover Art: Jay Aheer

ISBN: 978-0-3695-0018-2

HIS BEAST RETURNS

DEDICATION

For my readers.

HIS BEAST RETURNS

HIS BEAST RETURNS

Erin M. Leaf

Copyright © 2019

✒ ⋯ ◆ ⋯ ✒

Chapter One

Russell Kelvin looked up at the building, one of the taller glass monoliths in midtown Manhattan, and gritted his teeth. The owner of the building had named it and his company aptly, for he couldn't imagine a more forbidding tower of glass and steel. Monolith Enterprises owned the place, and Russell was here to step inside and back into the world of civilization after too long away. He hadn't set foot in the States in ten years, and he hadn't set eyes on Tristan Marik in even longer. His skin prickled with energy, and he swore he could taste electricity on the damned air, no matter how unlikely a scenario that was. He licked his lips, imagining Tristan's cool green gaze. Everything else would be different about the man, but not the eyes. Never the eyes.

"You can do this," he muttered to himself, like a madman. Only a crazy man would talk to himself in the middle of New York, but perhaps he *was* mad, despite how wretchedly sober he felt. People walked around him as if he were also part monolith, and it was true he was taller than average, but it was also true that in the city, people had places to be and he was simply an immovable object in the way of everyone at this time of the morning. He thought maybe he should've shown up later that day, perhaps just before five, and then his sudden appearance would've been unremarkable, except, well, he *wanted* to be remarkable. Tristan needed him to be remarkable. That was the whole point of this homecoming, after all. He ran a hand through his dark hair, knowing that no matter how carefully he styled it, people would be looking at the rest of his body long before they noticed his face. He hadn't bothered with a suit. It seemed pointless. He'd put on jeans and his boots and a black shirt, and if all of it showed his muscles just a little bit too well, so be it.

"You knew this was coming. You've known this was coming for over ten years now," he murmured, exhaling almost before he began moving forward. He pushed open the glass doors. The moment he stepped inside the cool, hushed foyer, the people behind the reception desk looked up, polite smiles fading as they took him in. He wasn't anything close to civilized, and this gleaming building wasn't anything close to the wild lands where he'd been living. His mother would say that he was a beast set loose in a china shop, and she wouldn't be too wrong. It was a pity she'd been dead since he was a child. She would've enjoyed this kind of homecoming. He would've enjoyed her enjoyment.

"Can I help you?" one of the women behind the gleaming desk stuttered, eyes riveted to his chest. A faint blush rose onto her cheekbones. The other woman's dark skin hid any blush, but he felt her attention on him just the same.

Blonde. Grey eyes. Marlie, his brain supplied as he met the first woman's gaze. He knew all the key employees here, even though they didn't know *him.* "No, thanks. I'm good," he said in a clipped voice, nerves getting the better of him. He could pretend to be civilized, but it would never feel comfortable. He glanced at the others. The woman on the far end didn't even try to hide her curiosity. The man in the middle frowned faintly, sensing competition where there was none. Russell had no interest in the women, or even the man. "I know the way," he said more gently, taking in the vaulted ceilings and columns.

Tristan's father had built this place, but Tristan had his hands all over the design. And *that* meant Russell knew everything there was to know about the building, all of its secrets and deficiencies, not that anyone except Tristan had a clue about that. It was a pity the building was the only thing Tristan had control over for the past decade. Russell wouldn't have had to stay away for so long if that hadn't been the case. *And now you've descended into self-pity*, he thought, angry with himself. *Just what Tristan doesn't need.*

Marlie stared at him, but he simply smiled as he strode past the large desk to the bank of elevators. "Wait! You can't go up without a security pass," she said, standing up. The man in the middle of the two women, as blond as Marlie, stood up, too. He looked less confused and more inclined to suspicion.

Hmm. Not completely stupid, then, Russell thought, not that it mattered. The man wouldn't be a problem for *him*.

"She's right," the man said, holding the desk phone as if it were a weapon. "And you certainly can't use that elevator. That's the VIP lift."

"There's no need to call security, Jon," Russell said, nodding at him. He ignored their whispers about his knowledge of their names. They'd find out the details soon enough. He lifted his hand and placed it on the palm scanner of the executive express elevator, the one that went directly up to the top three floors. The elevator Tristan used. The elevator Edmond Marik had used before his death a week ago. A moment later it beeped, and he tapped in the floor of the building he wanted onto the screen. The doors opened.

The woman at the far end paled. "How—"

Russell smiled, but he had too much to deal with right now to take the time to explain anything to her and the others. "It's okay. I promise," he told the trio, stepping inside. "I'm expected."

And he *was* expected, just not today. Or rather, not at precisely this time, because he hadn't been able to give Tristan a solid date of arrival. He'd been in the middle of nowhere when the bolt of grief and horror had woken him from a dead sleep, and he'd known it was time to go home. He hadn't stopped to communicate what he was doing. He'd simply *gone*. Or come. *Whatever*. He rubbed his face. The inside of his skull exhausted him, sometimes.

The doors closed in front of his face, and Russell inhaled slowly as he stared at himself in the mirrored doors. His eyes glittered with power, and he snorted. Of course they glittered. The closer he got to Tristan, the stronger he'd become. He wondered if Tristan could sense his proximity yet. His skin prickled, but he calmed his mind. Control was something he'd perfected over the years.

The doors opened, and he stepped out. There was no receptionist here, just a short hallway and a set of polished steel doors with the Monolith logo inscribed into the metal. His lips twisted. He still thought the logo looked like a geometric dick poking its way into the sky, but what did he know? He was just an uncultured beast, after all. He reached out and slapped his hand on the palm scanner set into the wall. The doors unlocked, and he pulled them open, slipping inside quietly. No one in the open concept office looked up, and he half smiled. *If you get this far, you belong here,* he thought, amused. That's how security worked in places like this. Of course, he didn't quite belong. Yet. It wasn't until he started walking that anyone began to notice his presence.

At the end of a line of desks, he turned left, heading towards the corner office. Tristan was in a meeting, but it wasn't an important one. Russell had checked. He had access to everything, including Monolith's computers. He couldn't *do* anything with that access, but he could see it all. Tristan had slipped him in under an assumed name years ago. He rarely spent any amount of time in places that had access to the internet, but he knew his way around when he did log in, which he'd done just that morning just after disembarking his flight.

Russell stopped outside the corner office's doors, staring in at the people inside through the glass. He thought there'd be some sign of the old man's death, maybe a few black cloths symbolically draped here and there, but there was nothing. *And perhaps that's not actually surprising at all,* he mused, still looking into the office. Tristan's father was a criminal, after all, and Tristan wouldn't care about mourning him.

Beyond the people in the meeting, floor to ceiling windows stretched wide. The weather front moving in over the East River hazed the city skyline until even the sharpest buildings blurred. Tristan stood with his back to the doors, talking to three men and a woman who sat on comfortable couches arranged around a low glass table. Laptops and tablet computers were haphazardly scattered on the table. Russell's gaze caught on Tristan's shoulders. He had his emotions and instincts locked down tight behind mental walls, but behind them, he could feel the beast roaring. From the way Tristan's head twitched for just a moment, Russell had a feeling his old friend could feel it, too.

"You can't go in there." A woman snagged his attention, rushing forward to stop in front of him, blocking his access into the meeting. "Do you have an appointment, Mr.—" She looked down at her tablet and then back up again, forehead creased. She looked nervous.

Russell took in the black hair scraped ruthlessly into a neat bun at the nape of her neck. The woman's blue eyes were stern, and he could sense her intelligence as if it were a wall of energy washing over him. He told himself to be gentle. He was always telling himself that. Sometimes it helped.

"Meredith, how nice to finally meet you," he said instead of answering her question. He watched her eyes widen in confusion. "I'm sorry that it's under such grim circumstances." He wasn't sorry, actually, but he knew enough to voice the polite words that greased conversations. He remembered Tristan's email when he'd hired this woman, and his hopes that her competence would help him offset his father's excesses. From what Russell could see, that hadn't happened as much as Tristan would've liked. Her eyes seemed haunted, but that could perhaps be the deaths. Death could make anyone question their mortality.

"Do I know you?" she asked, glancing into Tristan's office, and then back down at her tablet. "You're not on the calendar. Mr. Marik will be in his meeting for the next hour." A touch of apprehension colored her voice.

"No, he won't. He's almost done reassuring them that their business won't be affected by his father's death. And they'll get used to dealing with Tristan instead of Edmond. I know he's an entirely different animal, but it's for the best, don't you think?"

Meredith blinked up at him, wordless. Russell shook his head, wishing she didn't have to worry, but there was no help for it. Her day was about to get much worse. "And no, we've never met." He turned and opened the door.

"Sir! You can't—" she said, reaching for his arm, but Russell had spent the last decade learning how to avoid such things and neatly sidestepped her instinctive grasp. He stepped into the office. Tristan stopped talking in mid-sentence, head going up like a wolf scenting prey on the wind.

Russell smiled. Of course Tristan would know he was here, even with his back turned. He waited, ignoring Meredith's quiet protests. She would be worried Tristan would be angry. She might even expect to lose her job. After all, Tristan's late father would have fired an assistant for allowing an intruder to crash a meeting, and Tristan had spent the past decade carefully making sure that his father never suspected that he was anything but a chip off the old block. He watched the expressions of the woman and one of the men on the sofas blanch into fear for a split second, and then smooth over into careful neutrality. The other two men merely looked irritated, but Russell could scent the fear beneath their frustration clear as day.

Tristan slowly turned around. Russell's skin prickled sharply, electricity flashing across his body like sparks of static. It had been too damned long. His mother had warned him about this, before she'd died, but he'd been a kid. He hadn't understood that her stories weren't myths. His cock swelled, but he ignored it. There was too much at stake right now for him to let his libido lead the way. He clenched his teeth and waited for Tristan to *see* him. The moment their eyes met, another prickle of power seared through him, and Russell braced himself—for what, he had no clue. Tristan *wanted* him here. Tristan had told him so, in his last email two weeks ago. And hell, even if Tristan had told him to stay away, he'd have come. It was time. He knew it was time even before the email. What they'd done to each other as teens had assured him of that.

"Russell," Tristan said, a hard edge in his voice. Someone else might have flinched, but not Russell. That edge told him that Tristan wasn't anything close to composed, despite his calm expression, but before Russell could say a word, Tristan strode over.

Fuck it. Let them all get an eyeful. Russell reached out and dragged his friend into a hug that shook him to the core, and given the tight desperation of Tristan's grip, he obviously felt the same way.

"Welcome home," Tristan said finally, voice low and surprisingly soft. The edge had faded into a tired relief. "Thank God."

Russell exhaled shakily, wondering what the hell had happened to get them here. He wasn't ready to let go yet, so he held on, soaking up Tristan's strength. Edmond Marik, Tristan's father, was dead. Tristan was not. Russell never thought they'd see this day.

"Home," he said, then had to stop and clear his throat. He could barely breathe. He forced himself to let go, though he didn't want to, and he knew damn well Tristan didn't, either. "It's been too fucking long, Tris." He felt rather than saw the shock of the people watching them. He'd bet no one except Tristan's mother had called him by anything but his last name or "sir" for the past decade, let alone a nickname.

"It has." Tristan nodded. "But it couldn't be

helped."

Russell sighed. "I know." The wealth of knowledge honed by forced distance weighted them both down.

Tristan didn't smile, but Russell could feel the energy flashing between them. He gritted his teeth again, praying he wouldn't lose it. His beast wanted out. His control said *no*. After a moment, the energy ricocheting between them calmed a bit, and he inhaled slowly and carefully. Tristan smelled like coffee and smoke and ozone. He wondered what he smelled like to Tristan.

"Mr. Marik, I'm so sorry. He walked right by me," Meredith interrupted, sounding sick with worry.

Tristan turned his green gaze on her, and Russell wasn't surprised to see the warmth in his expression turn cold. "I will forgive you just this once, Meredith." She blanched. Tristan shook his head at her when she made to exit the office, and she stopped, hands gripping her tablet so tightly her knuckles turned white.

Russell pressed his lips together. He knew why Tristan was being a dick, but it didn't make witnessing it in person any more palatable. And, too, wasn't it time to cut out the act?

Tristan turned back to Russell. "Did you have any trouble getting in?"

Russell's eyebrows rose. "Of course not."

Tristan snorted. "Of course not," he echoed, almost smiling, but then he wiped his expression clean again and turned to the people on the sofas. They'd been staring at him and Tristan with varying degrees of shock. "Please excuse me, but I need to cut this meeting short." Tristan waved a hand towards the glass doors of his office, clearly asking them to head out.

Russell stepped to the side as the men and woman stood up and gathered their things.

"We waited two months for this meeting, Mr. Marik," one of the men said angrily, if a bit warily.

Tristan raised a brow. "So?"

The man scowled, but after a moment he backed down. "I'll have my assistant call and arrange another time for us to continue this negotiation."

"You do that," Tristan said. "Perhaps you should tell your assistant to prepare your contracts more thoroughly, as well. I'm uninterested in deals that benefit no one but yourself, Mr. Takahashi." He glanced at the man's briefcase. "Particularly ones that are so transparently greedy."

The man glared at him. "You're worse than your father."

Ouch, thought Russell. Tristan wouldn't like being compared to a man he'd hated with every fiber of his being. Mr. Takahashi would be lucky to get even a foot in the door of the building again, let alone into a meeting with Tristan.

Tristan smiled coldly. The energy in the room, not particularly warm before, plunged into a deep chill. Russell saw Tristan's assistant shiver.

Mr. Takahashi held Tristan's gaze for only a moment before backing down. "Very well, Mr. Marik." He gestured to his colleagues, and walked out of the office as if something had bitten him on the ass.

Russell sighed quietly. He'd known this wasn't going to be easy, but he'd hoped for at least a little more to work with. "Tristan."

His friend turned to him, and Russell felt power hit him square in the chest. To his amusement, the people watching from outside the office hurriedly turned back to their work.

"Open concept office plans are a terrible idea," Russell said, mildly. "No privacy." The cold energy

Tristan put out turned to heat the moment it brushed Russell's skin. His cock swelled more, and he knew his erection pushed up against the placket of his jeans where anyone could see. He made no effort to hide it. He wondered if Tristan's assistant noticed, but when he looked at her, she had her eyes on the floor.

"You didn't come all this way to discuss office decoration trends," Tristan said, shaking his head. He closed the door, trapping poor Meredith inside with them. He raised a finger, then tapped a spot on the glass. It immediately frosted over. "There. All the privacy you want." He turned to his assistant. "Come, Meredith." He strode over to the large metal desk set into the corner of the office.

Russell followed them over, interested to see how Tristan was going to smooth over the poor woman's terror. Tristan sat down and steepled his fingers together. "Meredith, I'd like you to meet Russell Kelvin." He glanced at Russell. "Russell, this is my assistant, Meredith Starson."

"A pleasure, Ms. Starson." Russell nodded at her, and then wandered around behind the desk to look at the view. He didn't trust himself enough to touch anyone. Not now. Not when his control was barely hanging on. "Three years, right?" He turned to see Meredith eyeing him warily. Every time her gaze landed on Tristan, it skittered away.

"Sir?" she asked, clearly confused.

"You've worked for Tristan for three years, correct?" Russell asked. He went over what he knew from her files. "Masters in Business Administration. Well-versed in contract law. Excellent at interpreting scientific literature."

She nodded warily. "Yes."

He looked at Tristan. His friend stared back at

him, not giving an inch. Russell perched on the edge of the desk. He'd be damned if he was going to pretend Tristan scared him. Meredith's eyes widened, but he ignored her dismay, turning to Tristan. "You realize we have to start somewhere. You can't keep this up."

Tristan sighed, shoulders relaxing slightly. "Do we?"

"Tris." Russell didn't need to say more. His beast clamored to be let out, but he ruthlessly shut it down. Tristan did not need him going feral right now.

"Shit, Russell. It's been a hell of a week." Tristan rubbed his eyes.

Russell knew that, but at this point it didn't matter. Tristan's safety came first. "I need her skills." Tristan frowned at him, and Russell reached out and touched the back of his hand. "*We* need her skills, and her goodwill. It's hard to do your best when you're terrified. You, of all people, should know that." Energy flowed through them and between them, clear and concise, and fucking incredible after all these years. Russell hadn't dared to hope their connection would still work properly, but, obviously, he'd underestimated their bond. He felt Tristan's grief over his mother's death, and his towering rage at his father, who'd forced him to do the one thing he'd hoped to avoid. And he was certain Tristan felt Russell's own sorrow over Julia's death— Tristan's mother had been kind to him when no one else had seemed to realize he needed it. It wasn't as if his own father had been a good man, after all.

Russell leaned back, breaking their connection, and Tristan finally nodded. "Fine. Whatever you say. I'm too fucking tired to argue with you." He rubbed the back of his neck as if it ached. It probably did.

"You won't regret it," Russell told him, watching Meredith from the corner of his eye. Her shock over his familiarity with Tristan was to be expected, and so was her surprise that Tristan could sound so human. Tristan had spent the last twelve years convincing everyone he was as evil as his father. Any sign of human emotion would be shocking. Meredith's reaction told Russell everything he needed to know. He could sniff out a traitor anywhere, and she wasn't one. She was an intelligent woman trapped in a job she'd never expected to turn into a cage filled with rats and sharks.

"Meredith, you don't know this, but my father and I didn't exactly see eye to eye," Tristan said carefully.

Russell reached out and put a hand on the back of Tristan's chair. His thumb brushed against Tristan's back, close enough to feel the warmth of his body, but not enough to trigger their bond. Just that little bit of touch helped. Tristan didn't say a word, but Meredith's expression told him that nothing about this was normal. Russell already knew that. Tristan didn't let people touch him, and this was the third time Russell had invaded his space in the past ten minutes. If she knew how badly Russell wanted to do more than simply hug his friend, she'd run screaming from the room. Russell bit back a smile. If *Tristan* knew, he kept the knowledge locked down.

"I don't understand," Meredith said nervously, still clutching her tablet. "How do you two know each other? Who *are* you?" she asked, gaze finally settling on Russell.

"Have a seat, Meredith," Russell said, gesturing with his free hand to the comfortable chairs in front of the desk. He ignored her question about who he was. God knew they'd have to explain eventually, but right now, *he* didn't know who he was to Tristan. Not really. A lot could change in a decade, and it had been longer than that since he and Tristan had made their bond with each other.

And, too, Tristan didn't really understand what he was getting into when we swore that oath, Russell thought, feeling that familiar prick of guilt. He hadn't quite known, either, but the responsibility for the aftereffects sat firmly on his shoulders. He hoped Tristan could forgive him, especially after all this time. *And all my silence.* Russell had never wanted to explain over email.

When Tristan nodded at her, Meredith slowly sank down. "When Russell speaks, he does so with my authority," Tristan said.

Meredith's eyebrows rose. "I don't understand."

"You know that my father's death was … unexpected," Tristan continued.

That's a hell of an understatement, Russell thought, but didn't let his emotions color his expression. Everyone thought that Tristan's mother had accidentally killed Edmond Marik while trying to put her husband's gun away in the nightstand, and that she'd then killed herself out of grief. Of course, everyone was completely, utterly wrong.

Meredith nodded carefully. "I know."

Tristan pursed his lips. "And you know that my father had many enemies."

Meredith nodded. "Yes." She frowned. "Are you trying to tell me that one of your father's enemies had him killed? And Mrs. Marik, too?"

"Not quite. What you don't know is that my mother was working with one of my father's enemies," Tristan said softly.

Half-true. Russell waited. If Tristan didn't come clean, he would force the issue. He needed Meredith on their side. Tristan glanced at him. Russell raised an eyebrow.

"Damn it, Russell." Tristan rubbed his forehead. "You can't expect the impossible."

"Yes, I can." Russell shook his head, frustrated. They didn't have all day. *Fuck it.* He couldn't stand this cat and mouse game anymore. "What Tristan is trying to say is that Mrs. Marik was working with the FBI to expose some of Mr. Marik's shady business deals, specifically his extremely lucrative business with a certain Venezuelan cartel. Mr. Marik found out and beat her to death, but not before she got her hands on his weapon and defended herself." He left out the part where she'd missed her shot. He'd take Tristan's involvement in his father's death to the grave. "Tristan found them like that."

"What?" Meredith whispered, hand on her throat. "Dear God." She swallowed several times. "I thought it was an accidental death and a suicide."

"No," Tristan said bitterly. "It was a murder-murder."

Russell looked Tristan. Tristan stared back, defiance in his gaze. "There was nothing you could've done," Russell murmured. He understood all too well Tristan's guilt, sorrow, and anger. He had quite a bit of his own to carry, after all.

Tristan stood up and walked to the window. "So you've said."

"Why are you telling me this?" Meredith asked, looking from Russell to Tristan and back again. Her closed off expression didn't bode well for the rest of the conversation. He knew quite well that Meredith and the rest of the people at Monolith believed Tristan was as evil as his father. Meredith hadn't been the least bit surprised when Tristan told her that the FBI was investigating. She was only shocked that Mrs. Marik had been working with them. She was likely terrified all over again. Knowledge like this could be very dangerous.

"People are trying to kill me, because word got out that my mother leaked information to the Department of Justice," Tristan said, still staring out at the city. "Because I've inherited everything." He waved a hand tiredly. "I've inherited my father's enemies and his crimes and his illegal deals. May he rot in hell. Some of the men involved in those illegal deals aren't particularly happy that I've already cut them off."

And he's also inherited the old bastard's money, and reputation, Russell mused, but did not say. "And so I've come home," he said instead.

"That's about as clear as mud," Meredith said, looking at Tristan's back. She'd seemed to have mastered her shock, at least for the moment.

Finally, some spirit, Russell thought, smiling. "I know you don't particularly like your boss, Meredith."

She gave him a look.

"Was that supposed to be a secret?" Russell asked, ingenuously. *Now, who's being cruel?* he asked himself. The smile slid from his face. "I'm sorry." She deserved better.

"Stop tormenting the poor woman," Tristan said, finally turning around. He leaned over his desk, resting his weight on his hands. "Meredith, we need your help."

She frowned. "I would prefer not to be involved in anything illegal."

That was when Russell knew this dancing around the truth had gone too far. "Tristan would never ask that of you."

She pursed her lips, but didn't respond.

Tristan sat down, glancing at Russell. "Everyone thinks I'm the same kind of man as my father. You can't change that with a simple request and a little bit of information, Russell." He laughed angrily. "I played the part a bit too well."

"Stop it, Tristan. We'll walk through this mess, but you need to stop fighting my help." Russell looked at Meredith. A hint of surprise appeared in her gaze. *She doesn't understand who I am to Tristan,* he mused, wondering how to get her to trust them. "Tristan is nothing like his father," he assured her, but then her expression hardened and he knew that he hadn't succeeded in getting her help. Yet. *Damn it.*

"Mr. Marik, if that will be all, I need to be getting back to my desk," she said, suddenly standing up.

Tristan looked at her.

Meredith paled a bit, but didn't back down.

Interesting. She didn't look like a woman who was afraid of her boss any longer. Russell decided to take that change in attitude as a good sign. "We'll talk again," Russell told her.

She glanced at him, expression unreadable, then pivoted and marched to the door.

"You'll be getting a twenty percent raise in your next paycheck, Meredith," Tristan said, just before she put her hands on the door.

She spun around. "You can't bribe me into believing you." Her voice shook. "I've worked for you for three years. I know what I saw. I know what you *did*. Actions speak louder than words."

"True. And you've never once witnessed me abusing anyone, or engaging in illegal business practices." Tristan shook his head. "I'm not bribing you. I've been trying to give you this raise for a while, but my father always shot it down." He pulled his laptop closer and tapped a few keys. "You now have access to all of the payroll data and my business email, as you should've had since you've been working here as my assistant. See for yourself." He folded his hands together. "I'm willing to trust you with this, if you're willing to meet me halfway."

Meredith stared at him for a moment, then nodded sharply. "Very well. I'll check the email." She slipped out, then, clearly at the end of her rope.

Russell watched the door snick shut, then turned to Tristan. "She'll come around."

Tristan stared at the door. "I know. I can sense it. She wants to believe us." He sighed. "I'm so fucking tired of this, Russell. All the lies. The pretending."

Russell reached out, not sure if he wanted to risk touching Tristan again, but unable to stop himself. "Tristan." He touched a finger to Tristan's wrist. Just that much set his beast to growling again. His cock swelled, heavy and needy.

Tristan went rigid. Energy sparked between them. "Fuck, Russell. What the hell? How is this even possible, after all this time? How can we still feel this way? We haven't even set eyes on each other in over a decade." He leaned over the desk and put his face in his hands, but he didn't shrug off Russell's hand.

"Texts and emails aren't the same as being here in person, but my emotions were never in doubt." Russell slid his fingers up and cupped the warm skin of Tristan's neck. The energy quieted a bit, as if sensing his exhaustion. He still wanted to grab Tristan and hold him until neither of them could tell where one began and the other ended, but it had been years since they'd last spoken in person. And it had been over a decade since they'd shared that one, fateful kiss. A hell of a lot had happened in that time. "When was the last time you slept?" Russell asked instead of dragging Tristan up and into his arms.

Tristan looked up at him. "Seven days ago."

Jesus. The night before he shot his father, Russell thought, unsurprised, but still dismayed. "Well, then. I think it's time you went to bed."

Chapter Two

Tristan watched Russell pack up his laptop and shoulder his briefcase as if it were the easiest thing in the world to do. "You don't have to carry those," he said, knowing he was reading more into it than he should. He was just so damned tired right now. He felt like he was moving through a dream world, and Russell would disappear as soon as he woke up.

"It weighs nothing," Russell said, taking Tristan's wrist again. He seemed to like doing that. Tristan liked it, too, which was why he didn't pull away. "Let me carry it for you, just this once."

"My stuff weighs a ton," Tristan said, thinking more of the responsibility that now pushed him down than a single, slim computer. He had to somehow extricate his father's companies from the illegal mess he'd made of them. He had to manage it without screwing up the lives of thousands of employees. And he had to avoid the government and the cartel's assassins out for his blood while he did it. Truthfully, though, those problems weren't insurmountable. He'd already begun the process, and he was used to dealing with his father's business disasters. What really worried him was Russell. They may have been close when they were young, but what did that mean for them now? *And I know there are things he didn't tell me*, Tristan thought, feeling almost drunk with exhaustion.

"I've got it," Russell said, eyes glinting. He slid his finger over Tristan's wrist until the tip touched skin. "I've got you."

"Do you?" Tristan shivered as he stared at Russell. He'd fallen in love with a boy over ten years ago. This man, though… He barely knew him. Russell stood in front of him, muscular and menacing and not completely civilized. Tristan had to steel himself to keep from grabbing. "None of this feels real," he said instead of giving in to his lust. He had no idea if Russell was as turned on as he was right now. His preternatural ability to read people's emotions seemed to be broken, or maybe he couldn't read Russell like that. He didn't know. All he could feel was this weird energy, rushing through them both. It felt both strange and familiar. *It's probably lucky I'm so tired, or I'd be freaking out right now.*

He concentrated, but Russell's energy felt like a vast wall despite their bond. The bond he'd never truly believed in. He sensed Russell's exhaustion, and his relief at being here, but he couldn't filter out any smaller emotions, and sometimes those were the ones he most needed to understand. He swallowed a sigh.

"I'm as real as you are, Tristan. You thought I'd just disappear forever?" Russell laughed. "Not a chance. I was going to give it a couple more years, and then come back anyway, your father be damned."

Tristan smiled briefly. "But are you sure you want to be here now?" He touched the button that unfrosted the office windows and gestured at the space. "This is no great prize." He glanced across the office. His employees were bent over their computers as if afraid to catch his attention, and the truth was, Tristan was okay with that, at least for now. He didn't have the energy to deal with distraught workers. "*I'm* no great prize," he said more softly.

Russell glared at him. "Just shut it, Tristan." He put a hand on the doorknob, but stopped before opening it. "You haven't been sending me fucking updates to Monolith's security systems and updates about key infrastructure, and updates about contracts and deals for the past ten fucking years for no reason. I'm here. I'm staying. Hell. I shipped my stuff to your fucking penthouse." He slapped a hand on the glass. "I've got access to everything. Even if you wanted me gone, I'd have access. There's no getting rid of me." He inhaled sharply, then let out the breath in a long slow exhale as he held Tristan's gaze. "And you know that there's no going back for us. There hasn't been since we swore that oath. We have a bond, whether you admit it or not. Why else are you so good at reading people? Where do you think that ability came from?"

Tristan watched in fascination as Russell's eyes bled from dark brown to amber. "Wait. You can shift just a part of your body?" he whispered, avoiding Russell's questions. He didn't want to think about his strange empathic ability right now. Everything suddenly felt too real, as if the past decade and change had been the dream and his real life had only just started a half hour ago.

Russell stared at him. "I told you I could. I told you years ago. If I'd known you wouldn't believe me, I would've found a way to show you in person long before today," he said, an edge of frustration in his voice. "You, of all people, should know who I am and what I'm capable of. It's because of you that I can do this." He pointed to his eyes. "It's because of me that you can sense *this*." He grabbed Tristan's wrists and pressed, hard. "I shouldn't have stayed away so long."

Tristan gasped as Russell's emotions crashed into him amid a maelstrom of energy. He couldn't make sense of them all, and he was too fucking tired to wrestle his way to understanding, so he wrenched his arms down, forcing Russell to release him. Russell glared at him for a moment, then took a step back. Tristan watched Russell's eyes fade back into a normal dark brown.

"You couldn't have come here, before now." Tristan found himself shaking his head, instinctively horrified at the thought. "You would've died if my father and his goons caught you here. You would've died if they'd seen you anywhere near me. The old bastard never fucking forgot that he saw us together. Even getting you a login for the Monolith computer network was a risk," he reminded Russell, still staring at his friend. Even with his eyes changed back to normal human irises, Russell looked like a hunter. Like a killer. He shivered as his cock hardened. *Talk about a turn-on.*

Russell continued as if Tristan hadn't spoken. "Tristan, I have your DNA permanently inscribed onto my fucking bones. That's what happened when we mingled our blood together." He held up his hand, showing the silver scar that matched the one on Tristan's palm. "It's there forever, thanks to what we did, and you know it as well as I do, even if we've never discussed it. Even though I never really explained it." He sighed. "And I don't give a fuck if your father saw us kiss. I don't give a fuck if you've screwed a hundred women since that night. It happened. It was real." He visibly gathered his composure as Tristan watched. "If it wasn't real, then nothing my mother taught me was true, and I can't believe that. I just can't." He swallowed. "You and me, Tristan. Our bond is the only true thing in my life."

Tristan licked his lips. He heard Russell loud and clear. He even agreed with what Russell was saying, but he couldn't seem to wrap his mind around the words when what he was really fascinated by was how fucking hot his friend looked. He'd met Russell fifteen years ago. Russell had been fifteen to Tristan's eighteen. Neither of them had been full-grown, but now…

Now we're both a long way away from innocence, Tristan reminded himself, thinking of the past week. The past twelve years. He'd done a lot of horrible shit he wished he could forget, but Russell obviously didn't care. Russell stood in front of him, strong and determined and oh so fucking perfect. Tristan's body liked this very grown-up version of Russell, but his mind wasn't ready. His mind told him that he didn't believe he was free yet. He wasn't that optimistic. He remembered Russell as a lanky teen, and he remembered the terror he felt when they both realized they'd somehow bonded with each other, but the energy between them felt different, now. Stronger. Weirder.

"I think I need sleep," he said instead of addressing what was really happening. "Let's go home. I can't think straight anymore." He gestured to the office.

Russell looked at him, then unexpectedly smiled. "You've never been straight, Tristan." He opened the door.

Asshole, Tristan thought, half amused, half terrified. He marveled at his friend's ability to put his frustration away. *If only I could do the same.* He followed Russell out into the office, ignoring the whispers of his staff. They'd never seen Russell before, and they'd never seen Tristan act so casually intimate with anyone, except for his mother.

"I've been straight my whole life, Russell," he said in a low voice, ignoring his friend's skeptical glance. He'd hated it, but he'd had no choice. The only way to mitigate his father's horrors was by navigating the shark-infested water, every day. And to do that, he'd needed every tool he could muster to convince his father of his loyalty, and that meant women. Lots of women. "And so have you," he added, bitter but resigned. He knew neither of them had been monks these years apart. *And you're assuming there's still a we, Tristan. Maybe Russell doesn't want that from you anymore. Maybe he's just here out of loyalty and friendship,* a voice in the back of his head tried to whisper. *Maybe you don't want that anymore.* Jesus. He was going to give himself mental whiplash. The inside of his head was a mess.

Russell stopped in front of the elevators. "No, I wasn't a monk, but none of the people I screwed around with meant a damn thing to me, no more than those women meant to you. And I gave up the pointless fucking over five years ago. I had more fun with my own right hand than I ever did with someone else." He slapped a palm on the reader. The device beeped, calling the lift. "None of those people were you."

I guess that means there's still a possibility he wants this. Wants me. Tristan looked away. He couldn't let himself zone out on Russell's perfect body and perfect anger. He hadn't had the luxury of celibacy with his father breathing down his neck, wanting the perfect, heterosexual heir. "We should stop in the security office. Chesterfield needs to meet you in person." The elevator dinged, and the doors opened as he struggled to force his brain into the logistics of fitting Russell into his life.

Russell waited until Tristan walked in, and then he followed. "I don't know what's going on in your head, Tristan, but I wouldn't be here if I didn't want to be here. You know this." Russell tapped the display. The doors shut, and the lift began to descend. "We made that decision years ago. We wrote it in blood."

"You may regret coming home," Tristan said, thinking of his life. He hadn't been nearly as successful at stopping his father's illegal activities as he'd hoped, and as a consequence, Tristan's hands were dirty. He wasn't some naive teen anymore.

"Only if you *make* me regret it," Russell said.

Tristan looked at his best friend. His soulmate. His fucking salvation, and tried to be optimistic, but the truth was, he wasn't a good man. He was a damned killer. "I'm going to make you so dirty," he said, letting a hint of his grief bleed into his voice.

Russell smirked, deliberately misinterpreting Tristan's meaning, the bastard. "I hope so."

****

"Mark Chesterfield, meet Russell Kelvin," Tristan said, sauntering into the control room of Monolith tower. Most of his arrogance was fake, but appearances mattered. His lack of sleep, dead father, and desperation for silence didn't, so he let habit carry him into the room. A stern, middle-aged black man straightened up from the console he leaned over, gaze landing on them. Tristan nodded, seeing Mark's immediate understanding of the man he'd just introduced. "Yes. This is the guy I gave full access to, behind my father's back. Yes, he's real."

"Russell Kelvin. I thought you were a myth," Chesterfield said, walking over with his hand outstretched. The two other security guys in the room watched them, identical expressions of skepticism on their faces, and Tristan barely controlled a scowl. They had no right to judge. So what if Russell looked like a hippy hiker? He was a hell of a lot more than that, as they'd soon learn.

"Let's take this into your office," Tristan said after Russell and Chesterfield shook hands. He felt a shiver of energy from Russell, and a strong wall of nothing from Chesterfield. He'd been able to sense people's emotions for years now, but the ability wasn't as stable as he'd like. Sometimes he even questioned whether it was real, but with Russell here, everything felt magnified. Anything seemed possible.

Or maybe that's my exhaustion talking. When it came to Chesterfield, Tristan figured the man had learned how to shield his emotions because he rarely felt anything from him without pushing. Tristan glanced at Russell to find him staring at Chesterfield the way a dog contemplated a bone. He hoped the two men got along. He needed them to get along. Besides his mother, Chesterfield had been the only ally he'd had in the ongoing, invisible war with his father. He touched Russell's arm, and then led the way into Chesterfield's small office, set off to the side of the larger security room and shut the door.

"I'll be honest, I thought Tristan had me set up your access because he wanted an extra login," Chesterfield said, leaning back against his desk.

"Why would I want another login?" Tristan asked.

Chesterfield shrugged.

Russell looked around the small room, but Tristan could've told him there wasn't much to see. Chesterfield barely used this space. His computer dominated his desk, but aside from a lone filing cabinet, the room had no personal touches at all. Tristan knew Chesterfield deliberately chose austerity in order to keep Tristan's father from learning too much about him, but the man didn't realize Tristan was the one he needed to be wary of. Tristan could ferret out any secret if he focused properly. That's how he known Chesterfield was trustworthy. He'd investigated the man himself, back when he'd hired him.

"No, Russell is quite real. He's always been real," Tristan said, not sure if he was trying to convince his security chief or himself.

Russell finished casing the room, gaze lingering on the blank walls, then turned his attention to Chesterfield. "I would like to go over your emergency protocols for this building tomorrow. Tonight, if you could send me a copy of Tristan's security detail, I'd appreciate it."

Chesterfield frowned. "I know you have full

access to everything, but that doesn't mean you get to review my methodology."

Tristan shook his head tiredly. "Actually, he does." He walked to the file cabinet and tapped it. "Every suggestion I made to you about security came from Russell."

Chesterfield stared at Tristan, then stood up slowly. "Are you asking for my resignation? I've been a security expert for longer than you've been alive, Mr. Marik."

Tristan hesitated, then looked to his friend. He wanted to see what Russell would do, but Russell merely exhaled, running a hand through his hair. "No. That's not what I want." He tipped his head at Tristan, lobbing the conversational ball back to him.

Tristan sighed, knowing that Chesterfield saw Russell as a young unknown, and that Russell didn't feel comfortable making that kind of decision without more time. Chesterfield had no idea what Russell could do, and the situation wouldn't let them learn about each other slowly. "You can trust him, Russell. He's loyal to me, not my father," Tristan finally said. He trusted that Russell could feel his sincerity. Chesterfield ... well. He had no idea how the man would react. He'd been touchy since Tristan's father had died, and that was saying something.

"Is that supposed to reassure me?" Chesterfield asked Tristan, eyes bright with irritation. "You're as dangerous as Edmond Marik ever was." He shook his head. "What's really going on, Tristan? You hired me to supervise security at this building, and then I assisted you with some extra work, but you've never explained what you really wanted." He crossed his arms. "And I know that you have some sort of ulterior motive. You wouldn't have hired me right under your father's nose, otherwise.

His old security chief hated my guts."

"The late, unlamented Vincent?" Russell asked quietly.

Tristan nodded, wondering if Russell thought he'd killed him. He hadn't. Vincent had slipped going down the stairs and hit his head six months ago. Tristan suspected his father had pushed the man, but he had no proof. His father had a habit of disposing of people he thought had outlived their usefulness, and Vincent had failed the old man one too many times. Tristan ran a hand over his face. "I fired Vincent's men as soon as I could, but that doesn't guarantee loyalty among the remaining personnel, nor does it help me with my own safety. And of course, now we're short-staffed."

Russell put a hand on Tristan's arm. Energy flared again, like a jolt of caffeine to Tristan's system. He breathed in slowly, brushing the fog from his mind. "I'm all right," he murmured. Russell let go.

"Who are you loyal to, Mr. Chesterfield?" Russell asked.

Tired as he was, it was easier to let his control relax than to keep a lid on it, so Tristan let his mental walls thin. Mark Chesterfield was a retired military security specialist, and he had a hell of a poker face, but no one could hide from Tristan forever. The energy he shared with Russell was stronger now that he was home, and he used it. He let his senses unfurl, tasting the air as Chesterfield's mind opened to him. He saw confusion and uncertainty, but also a rigorous set of ideals spooling through the man's thoughts. He nudged, just a little, and the man relaxed. Tristan pulled his energy back.

"I'm loyal to you, Tristan," Chesterfield said, quietly. "You know this. You hired me. You interviewed me." He paused. "You protected me from your father."

Tristan nodded, remembering that day when he'd

covered for the guy. His father had been ready to fire Chesterfield, but Tristan talked him out of it. Chesterfield had been home, caring for his sick wife. At any other job it would've been a normal personal day, but Tristan's father had never been particularly kind. "You can trust Russell, Chesterfield. And I think you'll be surprised when you find out what he can do."

Chesterfield rubbed his chin. "Fine. I'll send you the info you want, but I want something from you."

Russell tilted his head. "What?"

"Respect. I've been handling the aftermath of Mr. Marik's death for the past week, and weeding out the bad apples in Monolith security. I haven't slept more than four hours in a night. I deserve your consideration, Mr. Kelvin," Chesterfield said, voice firm.

He's never been disrespectful, Tristan thought, annoyed, but then he realized that Chesterfield was trying to establish his authority. *If only he knew...* Tristan held back a laugh.

"Of course," Russell said, as Tristan knew he would. "I have no intention of displacing you. I have no interest in anything except keeping Tristan alive."

Tristan watched Chesterfield's expression go from determined to speculative. "Thank you," Tristan said hurriedly. He had no desire to get into a conversation about his personal life with the man. *Not now, and hopefully not ever.* He turned to Russell. "Are we done here?"

Russell nodded. "Yeah. Time to go home."

Chapter Three

Russell followed Tristan back into the elevator. "You look like you need to sleep for three days."

Tristan laughed. "Yeah. I feel like it, too." He palmed the security panel, then tapped the icon for his penthouse. "Your stuff arrived a couple days ago." He smiled wryly. "The staff was very confused when I had them put it all in my bedroom."

"It's only a couple of bags. I hardly own anything," Russell said, feeling awkward now that he didn't have to put on a show for Tristan's people. He hadn't been back home in a decade, and this building hadn't even been built when he'd left. The last time he'd been in North America he'd stayed on the west coast. He wasn't even sure where *home* was anymore, except it was wherever Tristan happened to be. "Your room?"

Tristan shrugged.

Russell leaned back against the wall. He wanted to grab Tristan and hold him until they both forgot about the past twelve years. *But he's grieving his mother. And possibly his father, even though he'd never admit it,* he told himself.

"I can feel you thinking," Tristan said, sounding tired. "Stop it. I'm not missing my father any more than you missed yours when he died, so you can cut that right out."

"You can feel *everyone* thinking," Russell replied, not about to deny his worry and frustration. "And you may not be missing your father, but you're sure as hell missing your mom, and the situation isn't what I'd call ideal."

"True." Tristan closed his eyes and leaned his head back against the wall. "But I don't want to talk about it. You're back. That's a good thing."

Russell cut him a break. "And you missed me."

"Of course I missed you, dumbass." Tristan smiled briefly, and then the doors opened. "Welcome home," he said, shoulders relaxing. He pushed off from the wall and led the way out of the elevator.

Russell followed him into a beautifully decorated space. "Damn. This is amazing." Tristan's penthouse looked like something out of an architecture magazine: vast open spaces, white floors, a wall of windows showcasing the East River. Something about it eased the pinch in his soul that had twisted tighter the further into the city he had to go. "Did you have anything to do with decorating this place?"

"Sort of." Tristan shrugged. "I told them I wanted peaceful colors. I vetoed stupid designer shit. This was what we came up with."

Russell snorted. "So they chose white and pale blue. That's oddly serene, considering I remember the disaster that was your teenage bedroom." He followed Tristan past the formal living room, through the kitchen and family room combo, and down a wide hall. Tristan pushed open double gleaming wood doors and led him into a master suite. "And lavender, of all things," he said, taking in the almost but not quite grey comforter on the king-sized bed. The pale purple glimmered in the light of the late afternoon sun. The room was set into a corner of the building, and one wall of windows faced west, while the others looked south. The furniture was warm wood with tasteful steel accents. He felt himself relaxing even more.

"My father never lived here, so I got to do what I wanted with the place," Tristan said, pointing to two beat up duffels slouched against the wall. They looked completely out of place in the midst of all the gleaming minimalism. "There's your stuff."

Russell walked over and crouched down, palm on top of the nearest bag. He could feel his laptop in the front pocket, and he hoped the padded bag he'd stored it in kept it safe. "You want me to take the guest room?" He knew there was one across the hall. He'd seen the plans for the building before it had been built, and he'd seen the updated versions. He knew where the safe room was, and the emergency stairwell, and the secret elevator. Tristan had used quite a bit of money and manipulation to keep that particular specialty item a secret from his father.

"Do you *want* to sleep in the guest room?" Tristan paused, hand on his undone tie. He looked exhausted. And annoyed.

Russell made a quick decision. "No, I don't. I'll stay here with you. You need rest. So do I." He knew they'd both sleep better if they were together. They'd been apart for half their lives. He didn't want to pretend that hadn't left a mark on his soul. Tristan might not know the extent of their bond, but he sure as hell could feel the effects.

Tristan nodded. "Good." He tossed the tie on the floor and started shucking the rest of his clothes. He let his expensive Italian suit crumple into a pile near his feet. "I can't think. I feel like my brain is full of fog." He put his hands on his head, dressed in silk boxer briefs and nothing else. His sleek muscles bunched up under his skin.

Russell walked over and grabbed Tristan's wrists, trying to ignore his friend's ridiculously toned body. Tristan worked out, a lot. He always had, because he had nowhere else to put his natural aggression in the world he had to live inside. Russell's body was just as hard, but it was because of where and how he'd lived for the past decade. His cock filled as his gaze flicked over Tristan's smooth skin, but he ignored it. Tristan didn't have the capacity to deal with his lust right now. "You don't have to think. It's time to rest." He pulled him to the bed and nudged him down. "Under the covers," he said, prodding until Tristan rolled over. He tucked the comforter around him. "Sleep. I'll be here."

"Come to bed," Tristan said, grabbing him before he could move away. "I feel better the closer you are, and if that isn't completely fucked up, I don't know what is."

"It's not fucked up," Russell said, rubbing his chest. His heart hurt. Deep inside, his beast grumbled, wanting out. He needed to talk to Tristan about their bond, but now wasn't the time. "I will. I need to wash the stink of traveling off me, first."

He'd spent the last twenty hours in airports and on two separate planes. He'd been in northern India, in the middle of nowhere, when he'd woken up *knowing* it was time to go home. By the time he'd made it back to a city with Internet access, Tristan's email about his parents' death had been waiting. It'd taken him almost five days to hike into civilization, and another two to get here. He wanted nothing more than to collapse into bed with Tristan, but he was starving. And worried that Tristan, even with his mental acuity, didn't understand had badly he wanted him. He needed to get himself under control.

Tristan nodded, eyes closed.

Russell ran a hand over Tristan's head, amazed that such a hard, difficult man could have such soft hair. Tristan kept his blond hair short, and for a moment Russell wished for the teenager he'd once known, the boy with the hair that flopped over his forehead and the sparkling eyes, but then Tristan sighed and Russell pushed the thought down. They couldn't go back into the past. They had to live in the here and now. There was no other option.

Food, then a shower, he told himself firmly, putting away his exhaustion and lust and regret.

****

An hour later, he slipped into the bed beside Tristan. He'd washed up, eaten, and gone over the email Chesterfield had sent, so he was completely up to date with Tristan's personal security plans. Whenever Tristan left the building, two men followed. Russell didn't know if that was enough, but he was here now, and he would die before he let someone hurt Tristan, so that had to be worth something. He'd had a few suggestions for Chesterfield, and he'd sent them off, not caring if the man liked what he had to say. It didn't matter, either way. Russell would protect Tristan with his life. Tristan's father hadn't been a good person. He had enemies who scented blood in the water, and Tristan had no intention of following his father into the mud. So, Russell was here, and here he'd stay.

"Mmm, Russell," Tristan mumbled, and Russell smiled as his friend grabbed him by the arm. He held on tight enough to leave bruises, but Russell didn't give a shit.

"I'm here," he murmured, not sure where to safely put his hands. He settled on gripping Tristan's wrist with his fingers as he let himself relax onto the too-soft bed. They'd kissed once, sure, but that had been a hell of a long time ago. And they'd shared blood, because kids did stupid things like swear blood oaths without understanding the consequences. If his mother could see him now, she'd be so angry with his cluelessness, but she'd died long before he'd grown up enough to understand that her stories were more truth than myth. He sighed, thinking of her words, and how she'd insisted that the blood they carried was magic. That their ancestors could shift into other forms. When he was a kid, he'd thought she'd meant it metaphorically, but he'd been so very fucking wrong.

And then Russell's father had started taking blood samples after she'd died, and the entire gruesome reason he'd married Russell's mother in the first place had come out. *Not soon enough to save me from his fucking ego, though*, Russell thought bitterly. Russell's father had worked for Tristan's father as a biochemist, and he'd used his own son as a source of raw materials. Russell's father had believed some of his wife's strange tales, and blood didn't lie, not that either of them had understood the true implications at the time.

Bonded, Russell thought, rolling the word over in his mind, and not for the first time. That blood oath with Tristan had changed him. It had activated something dormant in his DNA. It had activated something dormant in his blood, and then that blood had changed Tristan, too. Even over vast distances they were connected. Tristan might deny it, but he knew this truth just as Russell did.

"Stop thinking so loud," Tristan said groggily. His grip tightened on Russell's forearm. "I can't sleep with your emotions raining all over the place."

"I don't know how to stop," Russell said, meaning more than Tristan realized. He didn't know how to stop longing for his friend. His blood-brother. His lover? They'd never been lovers, but that was how he thought of Tristan. At least his father had never succeeded with his experiments. All that blood he'd drawn from Russell had been for naught. Michael Kelvin had died thinking none of his experiments had borne fruit, thank God, and he'd died shortly after Edmond Marik had walked in on Russell and Tristan kissing. That had been the end of Russell's normal life twelve years ago.

Tristan rolled over. "I don't want you to stop feeling what you feel. I just want you to know that you can let go, now. You're home. You can rest." His eyes gleamed in the dim light from the setting sun. It was summer, so sunset happened late, but Russell's body thought it was the middle of the night. Jet lag sucked. "Go to sleep, Russell," Tristan said, more clearly.

Russell swallowed. The tone of his friend's voice promised so many things, yet Tristan's energy pressed at him, prodding and pushing, keeping him awake. He sighed and let Tristan's gift wash through his mind. He didn't have anything to hide. "You need to rest, too, not go poking around in my brain."

Tristan sighed, relaxing as if Russell's tacit acceptance of his mental power had released some shackle from his body. "I know. So do you." He smiled as his voice faded. "You love me. I can feel it."

Russell rolled his eyes. Tristan's words had begun to bleed together in his exhaustion. "Duh."

"I love you, too," Tristan said, and then his grip went slack as he fell back into sleep.

"And isn't that a kick in the nuts," Russell muttered, trying to adjust his cock without waking Tristan. Sure, they loved each other, but it had been twelve years since they'd been together in real life. Twelve years was a long time. He wasn't sure what kind of love Tristan was talking about. He'd given up trying to find someone to fuck who wouldn't mind his obsessive attachment to a guy he'd known when he was a kid, but that didn't mean Tristan wanted him.

Or did it? Russell inhaled carefully. Tristan hadn't let go of his arm. His energy burned through Russell's body, as if the power they shared via their bond had strengthened again now that Tristan had relaxed into sleep. Russell hadn't expected the power to feel so alive. He closed his eyes. The energy felt good, like a warm wind rushing through him, soothing his beast. He could feel Tristan's mind slumbering, and he could feel his own power walking through his bones, and then edging closer to the surface than he'd like. He concentrated, reminding his body that he was the one in control here. He was *human*.

Shifting forms in his sleep had proven disastrous in the past. He wasn't about to let it happen tonight, while Tristan clutched his arm. His power was dangerous, and barely controlled, and he would die before he'd let himself hurt the one person in the whole world who actually mattered.

****

Russell groaned as he felt his skin contract and energy wash through him. He woke up all at once, panting from some dream where he'd been running or flying—he wasn't certain which. It took a moment for his eyes to work properly, but he thought it was morning, if the light slanting in from the windows wasn't another dream. That meant he'd slept the night through for the first time in he didn't know how long. He inhaled and held his breath, but his skin contracted again, and he rolled away from Tristan, exhaling hard. "Fuck." His beast wanted out.

"Russell?" Tristan sounded groggy. "What's wrong? What are you doing?"

"Stay away," he warned, crouching on the balls of his feet. The cold marble floor helped a bit, but not enough. Energy prickled at him. It had been too long since he'd let himself shift. His control had shredded.

"Oh shit." Tristan suddenly sounded awake. His head appeared over the side of the mattress. "You need to shift."

Russell stared up at him, teeth gritted. "Exactly."

"Let it go," Tristan said, looking alarmed. He'd never seen Russell change, after all. "You're safe here," he added.

Russell shook his head. Tristan didn't understand. He only had a few minutes, sometimes less, and then his beast took over, wrestling control of everything away from his human side.

"I'm not myself when I shift, Tristan. You know that," Russell said, gritting his teeth. Or maybe Tristan didn't know. He'd never seen it. They'd talked about it on the phone. They'd emailed. Because when Russell had needed to run in order to survive Tristan's father all those years ago, his abilities had been nascent. Now, though, they were anything but. He was a full-grown shifter. He was a throwback to another world. A more primitive world.

And Tristan is your bonded mate, something inside him said, but Russell pushed the knowledge down deep. Tristan was in enough of a mess right now. He didn't need Russell's instincts making things even more difficult for him.

"Everything is different now," Tristan said, sitting up. He leaned down, hand out. "You don't have to hide it from me, of all people."

Russell shied away, praying for control. "Jesus, Tristan. You can't touch me. Not now. We're bonded. That oath we took all those years ago changed us. Your energy feeds mine. Mine feeds yours. It's stronger when we're together. Surely you can sense that."

"I can, but that's a good thing, don't you think?" Tristan asked, eyes gleaming. "There's no need to worry about what you can do, now that you're finally back."

Russell stared at him, and abruptly the energy Tristan put out doubled. Heat shot through him and his control disintegrated as sparks of pain warned him that he had to shift or face the consequences. He'd tried to put it off before. Once. It hadn't been pretty.

"Russell?" Tristan frowned.

"Oh God," Russell groaned, clenching his hands into fists so tightly he was sure he'd break the skin. He wished what was happening was as simple as lust. He wished that he and Tristan could just fuck, like normal people, and get it out of their systems, and maybe love each other and do that for a while, but neither of them was normal. Because of that oath they'd taken, and his own cursed blood, they didn't get to do normal shit like that. He arched his back as arousal joined the pain, and wasn't that just fucking weird, and then his skin contracted again. He had to let go or lose himself.

"Brace yourself," he managed to tell Tristan, and then Russell exhaled, and it happened. In a blink of an eye, the beast at the center of his psyche flowed out over his human skin, and then he wasn't a man anymore. He had just enough control left to choose the form, but that was it.

"Holy fucking hell," Tristan breathed, staring at him.

Russell shook his fur out and sat down, vaguely unsettled. His wolf form wasn't prone to freaking out, which was why he'd picked it, so his unease was more of a low-level worry. Surprisingly, he retained enough of his humanity to realize that he'd never shifted that quickly before. *This is strange*, he thought, shaking out his fur again. The room looked different. Tristan looked different. His sense of smell told him everything he needed to know: Tristan was still tired, but lucid and powerful, and not the least bit afraid. Energy flowed through them. Between them. Someone was coming up the elevator with food. He turned his head and looked out over the city, then bit back a howl as he realized that there were no trees and no dirt for him to run through.

"Russell." Tristan was standing now, hand outstretched.

Russell huffed, then let Tristan touch his head. He waited for his human mind to retreat, for his sentience to disappear like it always did behind the veil of the beast, but nothing happened. If he were human right now, he'd be frowning, but as it was, his confusion came out in a series of growls.

Tristan laughed. "I told you it would be okay."

Of course, Tristan would know what he was thinking. That was his power, wasn't it? Russell tried to glare at him when his skin contracted again. He howled, and the sound changed to a screech. He flew up to the headboard and gripped hard. Claws sank into the wood. He had *not* planned on shifting again, but a bird was a better choice in this situation than a feral canine. Sometimes his instincts were useful.

"A falcon. That makes sense, even if you're bigger than the norm," Tristan said, nodding. "Better a hawk common to Manhattan than a wolf trapped in a high rise, anyway."

Russell felt less agitated in this form. He looked around, and his eyes had no trouble with the height or the city. When the elevator dinged, it took all his will not to fly for the window. The damned thing didn't open, and he'd bash his head on the glass if he let instinct take over.

"Our breakfast is here." Tristan slid out of bed and pulled on a heavy silk robe, black, of course. He looked like he was completely in control of himself and his surroundings. Russell knew better. Tristan was rested and calmer than he'd been yesterday, but his roiling emotions were firmly locked behind thick mental walls. Russell didn't blame him. The next few days were likely to be difficult. He watched him walk to the hallway. Before he could think about what he was doing, he was in the air. He landed on Tristan's shoulder and almost fell because he couldn't dig in to keep his balance.

"Whoa," Tristan said, putting a hand up to steady him. "I have no idea how I'm going to explain you."

Russell clicked his beak. He didn't care what Tristan told people.

"Fine. Everyone thinks I'm an evil genius anyway. Let them wonder how I tamed you," Tristan muttered, striding for the elevator. A bell rang again.

Russell settled down, wondering if he should try to shift back to human. He could lose the ability to think at any moment, and God only knew what would happen then. Usually when he shifted, he was in the middle of some wild place where it didn't matter that he lost his fucking mind for a day or a week before he'd shift back. Here? In a penthouse in the middle of one of the largest cities on the planet? Disaster waited.

Tristan unlocked the security on the elevator, and the doors opened. Two women with a food cart started off the lift, but then stopped midway when they caught sight of Russell on Tristan's shoulder.

"Don't worry. He doesn't bite," Tristan said, stroking Russell's primaries.

Russell clamped his beak shut. He *did* bite. He was a fucking falcon, for Christ's sake. He wanted to bite Tristan.

"He's huge," one of the women whispered.

"No worries." Tristan stepped back. "He's mine."

As if that will reassure them, Russell thought sarcastically. Tristan was well known for his ruthlessness.

The women ducked their heads and quickly unloaded their trays onto the table. Tristan thanked them, and they scurried out. Russell flew over to the kitchen island, landing on the back of one of the tall chairs. It was wood, so he dug in his talons with grim satisfaction, shredding the smooth finish.

"Those chairs cost five hundred bucks each," Tristan said, unpacking fruits and eggs and caviar. "And you're gouging the back of one as if it was your own personal stress ball." He shook his head.

Since he couldn't roll his eyes in this form, Russell dug his talons in harder. Tristan could afford to buy new chairs a thousand times over. And the caviar smelled really damned good. He blinked, wondering how long he'd be stuck in this form, but as soon as he thought about it, energy flashed through him again. A second later he stood next to the chair, human hands on the clawed back. He sucked in a shocked breath.

Tristan looked up from the food, surprise chasing across his face. "Whoa, look at you. I thought you had no control over your shifting? I thought you'd be stuck that way for the day, at least."

"I don't have control." Russell shook his head, confused as hell. "I didn't." He could feel his power sitting just beneath his skin, and he frowned. It felt different. Stronger. Calmer. He knew he'd be more powerful near Tristan. They'd figured that much out before he'd had to leave, all those years ago, but he hadn't expected it to be *this* different. "What the hell?" He reached out a mental finger, shocked when the energy swelled. He thought of his jaguar form, and the next thing he knew, he'd shifted again. He stalked over to Tristan and butted his head against his friend's hip.

"Damn, you're gorgeous. I like this form," Tristan said, hands on Russell's head. Tristan ran his fingers through Russell's ruff.

Russell bit back a moan, then shifted back. He

was standing right next to Tristan, with his friend's hands on his hair. "I don't understand why this is suddenly so easy." *And so difficult.* He reached out and gripped Tristan's fingers. If the man kept stroking him, he wasn't going to be able to keep from reciprocating. He wasn't a damned *pet.*

Tristan shrugged, tugging his hands free. "We're stronger together. That's not surprising, right? You told me this bond thing would grow stronger with time. That's how it worked in your mother's stories, right?" He smiled crookedly. "We just didn't have the opportunity to experience it until now." His gaze flicked down to Russell's erection, then back up. His face had smoothed into an expressionless mask. "Maybe you should go put something on." He turned his back on Russell, shoulders tight.

Fuck. Russell stepped back as heat rushed through him. He was nude. That was normal, after a shift. What *wasn't* normal was being here, in a city, in full possession of his mind and Tristan not five feet away. Sadly, even embarrassment couldn't dampen his arousal. "I'm sorry." He turned on his heel and headed for the bedroom. He needed a cold shower and clothes and a few minutes to himself before he did something he'd regret, like grab Tristan and kiss the hell out of him.

Chapter Four

Tristan cursed under his breath as he watched Russell disappear. He sensed his friend's lingering arousal, dampened by embarrassment and pain. "And that's *your* fucking fault," he muttered, scrubbing a hand over his face. He'd panicked when he'd seen Russell's cock swelled thick and heavy against his abdomen. Arousal had hit him like a bolt of lightning, and he did what he always did when that happened: closed himself up. He'd been doing that for years, because his father hadn't believed in homosexuality, and if Tristan wanted to survive, he damn well had to repress what he felt. He was lucky he was more bi than gay and could function with women.

"The old bastard is dead. You don't have to play by his rules anymore," he reminded himself, trying out the words aloud. Maybe if he said them enough times it would stick. He flexed his fingers, remembering the way Russell's fur had felt. It was a miracle that his friend was still sane after everything he'd been through. It was a miracle that he'd come home. Tristan wished he could take back his hasty words. He was ashamed of himself for how he'd reacted. "Fuck."

He must have stood there for five minutes or more, because when he forced himself to move, Russell was already back. He'd put on jeans and another black shirt. He looked rugged and angry as he walked up to Tristan, who hurriedly fixed some food for his friend. Russell didn't say a word when he reached the kitchen.

No more than I deserve, Tristan thought. "Here, I made you a plate. Eat." He slid a platter full of caviar and eggs and toast across the island—an apology, of sorts.

Russell gave him a look.

Tristan flushed. He never flushed. "It's been a

long time since I've been with anyone. My father—"

"Your father is dead, and I hope he rots in hell with mine. The two of them ought to do well down there together," Russell said harshly. He picked up one of the crackers with caviar and ate it in quick, neat bites. "We need to talk about your parents' memorial service."

Tristan felt a tension headache slide into place along his neck. He supposed they weren't going to talk about what happened earlier, then. He couldn't say he wasn't relieved. "It's scheduled for tomorrow morning. My mother always wanted her ashes scattered at the beach, but you know that's not going to happen." He rubbed his eyes. "I'll be putting an empty urn into the mausoleum. What I'll do with her actual ashes, God only knows. I'll have to figure something out."

"You don't have to decide now. I'm sure we can manage a visit to a beach, health code violation or not," Russell said, as he picked up another cracker. "She was a good woman. We'll figure something out."

Tristan grimaced. He'd loved her deeply, and she'd been as trapped by his father as he had. "She saved my life."

Russell stopped eating. "Do you want to tell me what happened? I only know the barest details you gave me via text."

Tristan didn't want to tell him, but he knew he had to. Of all people, Russell deserved to know. "I'd gone to the house on Long Island to visit my mother, and as soon as I went inside, I heard screaming." He shrugged, pushing a cracker in circles on his plate. "That was nothing new. The old bastard yelled at her a lot." He glanced at his friend. "I know it sucked that your mother died when you were young, but at least she didn't have to deal with your father's obsession."

Russell sighed. "Maybe she knew. Maybe she

kept him from drawing my blood. Who knows what would've happened if she'd lived?"

Tristan sensed his sadness, and for a moment it nearly did him in. He knew what grief like that felt like, now. He swallowed, but forced himself to keep going. "So, I went to visit my mom, and I went to the bathroom as soon as I arrived, before they knew I was inside. When I finished, I headed to my mother's sitting room, and I heard my father yelling. I remember being surprised, because Mom told me he wasn't going to be home. I sure as hell wouldn't have gone to visit if I'd known he was there. I saw enough of him during the week." Tristan ran a hand through his hair. "And I stood at the end of the hall, wondering if I should go for a walk or maybe just leave, because it was more of the same shit. Nothing ever changed with them."

"It wasn't your fault," Russell said quietly. He didn't look angry anymore. "You know that."

Tristan started pacing. "I should have got us both away from him years ago. You know I tried a few times, but my father always tracked us down. We had to pretend we were on some spontaneous trip, like it was all a big lark." He made a sound in the back of his throat. His fucking father always found them. "I swear to God I think my mother let him find us. She always had this look on her face when he showed up. Half guilt, half dismay." Tristan shuddered. "He probably threatened her with my life. Wouldn't surprise me."

Russell grimaced. "What happened a week ago, Tristan? Why was she screaming?"

Tristan stared at his friend. Russell had shoved his plate away from him, and he stood there, shoulders tense. He looked … anguished. Tristan struggled with his mental walls. He could sense his friend's anger, and though it was terrible, it was only a drop in the bucket compared to his own. He couldn't tell this story if he had to shoulder Russell's rage as well as his own. He took a deep breath, and then another, using the time to shore up his control.

"Tristan?"

Tristan exhaled. "My father was hitting her with a fucking lamp, Russell. A lamp. I can't get the look on his face out of my head," he said, swallowing hard as the image of his mother's blood all over the floor flashed through his mind. "He was yelling something about the FBI, and she looked up at me, and I saw it in her eyes. I saw the truth. I know she went to them, and she wasn't sorry, either." He rubbed his face, suddenly exhausted all over again. "I don't blame her for going to the police. I wish she'd done it sooner. I would've helped her. God!" Tristan burst out, fists clenched. "Why didn't she ask me for help? Why the hell didn't she go to them sooner?"

"You had no idea?"

Tristan shook his head. "No. She never told me. She somehow managed to copy evidence from my father's computers, which is a minor miracle right there. The old bastard was paranoid as fuck. I wish I could've helped her." He slid his hands into his hair and tugged. "My father started hitting her again, and again, and I knew that this was it. He was going to kill her this time."

"This time? He hit her a lot?" Russell stepped around the island.

Tristan opened his mouth to respond, but Russell cut him off.

"Never mind. I can see the answer on your face. That fucking bastard," Russell said, voice low and hard.

Tristan knew exactly what Russell was feeling right now because he was feeling it ten times more strongly. He nodded, speaking past his anger. "Yeah. He liked to hit her. He stopped trying to hide it from me after you left." He choked out a laugh. "I'd stop him when I was around, but I couldn't protect her all the time without moving her out of there, and she refused to do that. This time, I could see he'd gone too far, so I went for the nightstand and damn the consequences. I knew he kept his Glock in there. The moment I got it out, my mother came after me and wrestled it out of my hands." Tristan swallowed, reliving that moment of heart-stopping anguish.

"Wait, what?" Russell's expression showed his surprise.

"I know," Tristan managed to get out. He felt like a hand was gripping his chest, but Russell needed to hear the rest, and he needed to say it. *Maybe saying the words out loud will help me get past this*, he thought, pushing past his grief. "I was too shocked to stop her. She hated guns. Never even fired one before," he said, letting some of the anger he still felt color his voice. "She lifted the gun and took aim at my father, and then she pulled the trigger and fucking missed. It was a nightmare." He looked at his friend. He wished they could go back to pretending that Russell was home just because, and not as a result of this completely fucked up situation. He wished he had the guts to tell Russell he still wanted him. Any unfinished business they had over their mutual attraction had been pushed aside in the face of this horrible situation.

"What happened next?" Russell asked, sounding almost afraid to find out.

"Next? Oh, it gets worse. Much worse," Tristan said bitterly. "After she missed, my father bashed her head in with the lamp. He was enraged." He shook his head, shuddering at the memory of his father's expression. "My mother collapsed like someone cut her strings, and I could see she wasn't going to get up again.

It was grisly. I scooped up the Glock and shot my father point blank in the heart." Tristan drew in a slow breath. This was the first time he'd said those words out loud.

And it's probably the last time I'll ever admit it to anyone, Tristan thought. Russell's gaze, thank God, remained steady, and Tristan knew right then and there that he'd do anything for this man. "My father deserved worse than what I did to him. He should've suffered the way my mother suffered." He slumped against the island, exhausted all over again. "Please don't ask me if I regret it. I don't. Maybe I should, but I don't."

Russell walked around the island and gripped Tristan's biceps. "I know you don't regret it. I wouldn't either. You did the right thing, Tristan." He stared hard at Tristan as if that would keep him from flying apart.

Tristan nodded, absently rubbing at his chest again. His bones ached. He thought he'd moved past this horrible sinkhole of grief, rage, whatever, but no. *I guess one week just isn't enough time to deal with this*, he thought, grateful that Russell was basically holding him up. He sucked in a shaky breath. If his employees could see him now, they'd never believe it. Most of them thought he was just as bad as his father had been. Cold and unfeeling. *If only they knew what a good actor I am.*

"What did you do then?" Russell asked gently.

Tristan sighed. "I put the gun back into my mother's dead hands, washed up thoroughly, and called the cops. It was easy. Too fucking easy."

"Nothing about this is easy, Tristan."

Tristan shrugged. If he tried to reply to that he'd lose it.

"The cops believed your story?" Russell hadn't let go of him. Tristan didn't mind. He'd swear Russell's hands on his arms were the only things keeping him anchored to the ground right now. "The cops?" Russell prompted.

Tristan shook his head and forced himself to answer. "They believed everything I told them. The housekeeper was off for the morning, and no one else was in the house, but they questioned all the staff anyway." Though it wasn't easy, he met Russell's steady gaze and held it. "The staff had seen my father beat her before. Like I said, it was nothing new." He shuddered. "Hell, they'd seen him beat me, at least until I hit him back that one time. It was just before you left, if you'll recall." Tristan remembered the incident well, but it still seemed like a lifetime ago. *Bad memories…*

"Jesus." Russell obviously remembered it, too. "That's crazy. You'd think he would've gotten the point after that." His hands dropped from Tristan's arms.

Tristan sagged without the support. "If you'll recall, my father was crazy. And he did business with crazy men. When he got into bed with that cartel, I just about had a stroke." Tristan had broken his father's nose the last time the old man had hit him. After that, his father hadn't raised a hand to him again because he'd figured out a better way to control him. All Edmond Marik had to do was threaten Tristan's mother, and Tristan would do whatever the hell the old man wanted. No one could ever accuse his father of being stupid. Crazy, yes. Dumb, no.

"I need to sit down," Russell muttered.

"The FBI showed up not long after the police arrived last week. It was a mess," Tristan said as he let Russell manhandle him into one of the chairs. "I was a suspect for a hot minute, but I guess the agent working the case with my mother knew enough to realize she was right up on the edge of losing it. God knew my mother told me enough times that she wished the old bastard was dead. Hell, she wished *she* was dead, and she wasn't afraid to mention that, either. My dad knew. I knew. *Everyone* knew she was on the verge of a nervous breakdown." He rubbed his eyes. His mother hadn't been a saint, but she hadn't deserved the life his father had given her. "It doesn't matter now."

"It does if the FBI is still investigating you," Russell pointed out.

"They're not. They already told me they'd closed the case." Tristan snorted. "I handed over everything they wanted. They think I'm a saint. I shut down all of my father's illegal businesses, and lawyered up for the rest of it. They can't touch me, and they know it."

"But other enemies can," Russell said quietly.

"Yeah. So they can," Tristan said, not surprised that Russell had hit the point directly on the head. He was a smart man. "The Venezuelan cartel in particular has a hard-on for me and Monolith. My actions destroyed a healthy heroin industry for them, not to mention a nice little side business in human trafficking. And my father was into something else with them, but I was never able to find out what. Something bio-pharmaceutical. Something lucrative." He suppressed another shudder. If he didn't start acting like he knew what he was doing, he'd never make it, and that meant *Russell* wouldn't make it, either. And Tristan refused to let anything happen to Russell. "They aren't happy with me. Maybe you should've stayed on the other side of the world. It isn't healthy to hang out with me right now." He stood up again. He couldn't just *sit* here and talk about this as if it was nothing. As if his mother's death was nothing.

"Don't be a fucking idiot." Russell stood up, too, and pulled him into a rough a hug.

Tristan resisted for a moment, but then he let his body relax. Russell smelled like warmth. He felt like home. And Tristan didn't remember the last time he'd let anyone touch him like this, except for his mother, so wasn't it time? Didn't he deserve some happiness? He wrapped his arms around his friend and held on, savoring the simple pleasure of an embrace without any ulterior motives. The women he'd had to fuck in order to appease his father's ego faded into the background. His sex life had been nothing but a transaction in order to keep up appearances.

Thank God I don't have to do that anymore, he thought, relieved, and then Russell hugged him tighter, and Tristan's cock twitched. He sensed Russell's sorrow and his love; even though Russell wasn't aroused right now, it didn't seem to matter. Tristan couldn't so much as look at him without wanting him, and what did that make him? Fucked up.

"I'm not the most stable of individuals, Russell," he whispered, thinking of how he'd pushed away the only living being who gave a damn about him not a half hour ago. And yet Russell was right here, offering comfort. "I'm sorry about before."

Russell shook his head. "Don't."

Tristan pulled away. He had to stand on his own, here, or he'd get them both killed. "It's just going to take a while." He ignored the erection he had from that little hug.

Russell pursed his lips. "I'm not going to let you get away with it, Tristan."

Tristan frowned. "Away with what?"

"Pretending you don't feel anything," Russell said.

Tristan walked around the island to the refrigerator. When he got there, he stared at it for a moment, before opening it and grabbing a bottle of water. He cracked it open and downed half of it before he turned around again. "I don't know what I feel right now,

Russell."

Russell sighed. "All right."

Tristan blinked. "That's it?"

"I'm not going to force myself on you," Russell said, rolling his eyes. "We're already bonded mentally. It's not like it'll be fun for either of us if you're miserable."

Tristan snorted. As if Russell could force himself on him. Tristan knew better than that. *Russell* knew better.

"Do you have to do any work today?" Russell asked.

Tristan shook his head. "No, thank God. I had Meredith cancel everything."

"Do you think she might help us?" Russell picked up one of the bagels and ate half of it in a few quick bites.

"I hope so, but she spent a lot of time with me and my father, so…" Tristan trailed off, making a so-so gesture with his hand. "She's got a lot to lose if she doesn't help. The cartel has to know who she is. I'm worried about my people, to be honest."

"Meredith saw you at your worst." Russell ate the other half of the bagel. "How you had to act in the past won't matter for long. She'll see the truth of who you are soon enough."

Tristan didn't know where the hell Russell found the energy for positivity. "Sure," he said, staring at the water bottle in his hand.

"You think I'm naive." Russell smiled. "Can't you feel it?"

Tristan looked up. Beneath his fingers, the plastic bottle felt cold and flimsy. "Feel what?" Most of the time he felt too much. He usually tried to keep it all out, except when he was actively using his power to influence someone.

"The energy, Tristan. How much stronger we are now that I'm here with you. I don't think I ever imagined it would feel like this." Russell walked over to him. "Give me your hand." The look on his face told Tristan that this would be different from the hug. "Please."

Tristan waited a moment, then did as Russell asked. The moment their palms touched, heat shot through Tristan. He bit back a moan. His mind opened up, and Russell's power rushed through him, hot and wild and familiar, even though he'd never sensed anything quite like it until Russell came home. Tristan shivered. "This is crazy. We're playing with fire, Russell, and we're going to get burned."

"I can handle a little fire," said Russell. His eyes glittered. "You realize, I could shift into anything right now? And when I changed shape earlier, I didn't lose my ability to think. I didn't even feel the edges of my humanity start to bleed away. Do you have any idea what that's like, after all this time?" Russell asked him, voice low and intense. Tristan felt the gritty heat of it deep in his body. "It's been twelve years, Tristan. *Twelve years,* and this is the first time I've felt remotely sentient while in animal form, and it's because of you."

He made to let go of Tristan's hand, but Tristan squeezed, holding tight before Russell could pull away. He didn't want to let go. He never wanted Russell to leave again. Even so, he had to make sure his friend understood the true nature of his mental state.

"I'm completely fucked up, Russell," Tristan said softly. "I know we're bonded somehow. That's obvious. We were young, clueless kids when we took that blood oath, and neither of us had any idea that what was in your blood would change me the way it did, but it doesn't matter now. I'm not normal. I'm not safe. I haven't been either of those things in years." Tristan wished they were young again, and that they could start over, and that he was anyone but who he was. *But my father's legacy is always going to be there, no matter how hard I try to throw it off.*

"Tristan—" Russell began, but Tristan cut him off with a grimace.

"No. We should try to figure out how to break the bond, not make it stronger. I don't want you trapped here with me." Even as the words fell out of his mouth his entire being protested them. He ought to set Russell free because it was the right thing to do, but he didn't want to. He wanted Russell in every way one person could have another, preferably naked and desperate. He stifled a groan just thinking about what that might mean.

Russell's eyes flashed. "After all these years and all we've planned together?" he asked tightly. "After the risks we took? No. Not just no, but *hell* no." He shook his head. "I'm not normal either, and I never have been. I never will be." He laughed, but he didn't sound amused. "My father was your father's evil scientist, Tristan. He experimented on his own kid. That's a horrible thing—as horrible as what your father did to you. My dad took my blood from me. He married my mother because he found out her family was somehow different. I'm as fucked up as you are. And there's no one else like us in the entire world. That doesn't mean we should try to break what holds us together." He moved closer, trapping Tristan up against the island. "And if you think I've spent the past twelve years of my life wishing I'd never met you, you'd be wrong." He reached up, and to Tristan's shock, cupped his face between his hands. "I didn't know what my blood would do to you, but I should have. I should have listened to my mother's stories, and understood what she was trying to teach me, but children never listen. And now I'm glad I didn't. I'm *grateful* we met and shared blood and bonded, Tristan. I wouldn't have it any other way. Can't you see that?" He took a deep breath. "Can't you *sense* that?"

The heat that flashed through them with Russell's touch almost brought Tristan to his knees, but he grabbed onto the granite counter behind him and held on with all he had. "Russell, you don't understand—"

Whatever he was going to say disappeared from his head the moment Russell's lips touched his. Tristan gasped, shocked and aroused and completely unbalanced, but Russell didn't seem to be nearly as confused as Tristan felt. He tilted his head and assaulted Tristan's mouth as if both their lives depended on this one, vital moment, and this one, vital connection.

And maybe it does, Tristan thought as he scrabbled at Russell's shoulders. His friend was hot as hell, and strong, and the most stable thing in his life, both now *and* in the past. He moaned, or maybe Russell did, he couldn't tell. All he knew was that Russell was finally *here,* and he was fucking *real* in a way that nothing and no one had ever felt before. He opened his mouth, and Russell's tongue slid inside as if he owned the place. Tristan tried to kiss him back, but Russell growled and bit his lip. Tristan choked as his ridiculously hard cock pressed into Russell's hipbone. "God," he tore his mouth away, gasping for breath. "What are we doing? This is crazy."

"If you think for one moment I'm going to let you shut me out like you do everyone else, Tristan, you're sadly mistaken," Russell murmured, hips doing a slow, devastating grind into Tristan's body.

Tristan could feel Russell's erection, thick and hot, and for a moment he wished his friend hadn't bothered with clothes, but then he remembered that his mother was dead. And it was his fault. "Wait," he said, when Russell lowered his head again.

"No. No more waiting. We've waited a damned lifetime already."

Tristan twisted his face away. "My mother just *died*, Russell. What the fuck are we doing, here?" He slid his fingers into Russell's hair and tugged, hard. The energy flowing between them didn't let up, and it felt like a tornado just about to sweep them away, or possibly a tsunami poised to smash them flat. He could barely breathe. He wanted Russell with a desperation he hadn't realized he had.

Meanwhile, Russell's eyes had shifted from dark brown to golden amber. He stared at Tristan unblinkingly, and with intent. Suddenly, Tristan realized that his friend wasn't entirely human. Tristan inhaled, more aroused than ever, and then he tried to shutter his mind. He'd somehow cast his power wide open, and everything he felt rushed through him and into Russell in a wild, volatile exchange of energy. He grabbed the doors of his mind, and he tugged hard, trying to close up tight again, but Russell growled. His mental presence chased away Tristan's resolve.

"Oh, no you don't," Russell said, thrusting a leg between Tristan's. "Don't you shut me out now." This brought their cocks into contact, and Tristan shuddered. Even trapped behind his jeans, Russell's erection felt like perfection shoving against his. He'd never felt so perfectly turned on. He gave up trying to shut away the energy and let Russell kiss him again.

"Yeah. That's better. Give it to me," Russell muttered, biting at Tristan's lip, and then down his jaw. "Fuck, this is insane. You drive me crazy, do you realize that?" Russell demanded as he slid his hands inside Tristan's robe. When his fingers touched Tristan's skin, they both shivered. "And yes, I know your mother died, but would she want you to keep putting your life on hold? Especially now?" He dragged his lips along Tristan's neck. "How much longer do we have to wait, Tristan?"

Tristan stared at him. Somehow, Russell had hit the nail squarely on the head. His mother had never wanted him to lock himself into the box his father had created for him even before she'd died, and she wouldn't want him to do it to himself, especially not now, when no one could hurt her any longer.

"No, she wouldn't," Tristan told Russell, hips grinding against his friend's. His power was wide open and surging wildly, and his ability to think had all but disappeared. "But you've only just come home."

"So what?" Russell asked him. "I'll be damned if I'm going to stop." He punctuated his statement with a devastating roll of his torso. "Not now. Not ever again." He put his head close to Tristan's. "I want to strip you naked and bite you and fuck you senseless, Tristan. I've been waiting my whole life to touch you."

Jesus God. Tristan gripped Russell's ass and squeezed, hard. If they kept this up, he'd come without anyone even touching his cock. Crazed with need, he fumbled Russell's pants open, cupping his erection when it pushed out over the zipper. He could barely believe he was here, touching Russell like this. Except for the one kiss he and Russell had shared all those years ago, he hadn't ever been intimate with a man. It felt … good. Too good. "So hot," he whispered, fingers surrounding Russell's cock as if he could memorize the skin.

"I'll show you hot. Stroke me harder," Russell said, hips moving faster. "Tighter. I don't mind a little pain." With a sudden move, he grabbed Tristan's robe and yanked it off.

Tristan's skin burned, and so did his mind. Energy rocketed through them as if they stood in the center of an electrical storm. Russell's eyes had bled to amber, and Tristan could see the echo of his beast inside.

"Touch me back, Russell." Tristan gripped Russell's erection firmly enough to bruise, wanting it in his mouth. Wanting it in his body. "Please. Just … touch me." He'd never wanted anything so acutely, not even through all those long years of hiding himself in plain sight. He wanted Russell, not just because of the sex, but because his old friend was the only living being who saw him for who he truly was.

After a moment's heart-pounding hesitation, Russell reached down and roughly groped Tristan's balls, then stroked a hand over his cock. "All right. Come on. Come for me," he said, moving his hand up and down. He wasn't gentle. He wasn't easy, and Tristan loved it. He loved Russell. He always had. Pre-cum coated the tip of his shaft, and Tristan groaned as Russell thumbed over the moisture, rubbing it in. He wasn't kind about it.

Tristan didn't care. He didn't need gentle. He didn't *want* gentle. He wanted it to hurt. "God," he burst out, hips thrusting forward into Russell's perfect grip. "Russell. Do it harder." He found Russell's cock with his hands and stroked him mindlessly, not even trying to do it with any finesse. He had no finesse in him anymore. He had only want and need and power, and the harder he pressed, the more Russell gave him.

"Fuck," Russell said then, very clearly, and then he climaxed all over Tristan's hand and groin. The heat of it sent Tristan over the edge, because he could feel how good it was. His mind was open. Russell's pleasure was his pleasure, and when his orgasm took him, he thought he might die of it before it let him go. He released Russell's softening cock and grabbed onto his friend's arms instead, hips working furiously. Russell staggered, and Tristan let go with one arm to grab onto the counter—

"Jesus Christ," Russell said, with the tone of a man who had no idea what was happening.

Tristan groaned, and his erection pulsed, and then the pleasure peaked. He shuddered, leaning on his friend. Russell wouldn't drop him. Russell wouldn't let him go. Russell held onto him just as tightly as Tristan needed.

"I've got you," Russell said, arms like steel around him as Tristan shivered through the last waves of pleasure, and those words were exactly what he needed.

A long moment later, Tristan snorted, completely unable to help himself. He felt like someone had taken his skin off and put it back on again inside out. The world was upside down. He slumped against Russell, then wrapped his arms around him.

"Not Jesus. Just me, Russell. It's just me." And God help them both, because Tristan had no idea what it meant that he'd just mauled his best friend. His *male* best friend.

"So it is," Russell said softly. "And that's okay."

Chapter Five

It took a supreme act of will for Russell to disentangle himself from Tristan, but it had to be done. He sensed Tristan's astonishment and love, and even though he felt the same, there was no way he could maintain that level of heightened emotion. There was no way *anyone* could maintain it in this particular situation, and Tristan definitely didn't have the energy for it right now. He hugged his friend, and then he stepped back, wincing as the drying semen that had begun to glue them together tugged at his pubic hair.

"Well, then," he said, like an idiot. He reached over to the sink and grabbed a handful of paper towels, wetting them almost absently. After he'd swiped at himself, he handed the wad to Tristan.

Tristan blinked at him, then smiled. "You realize that you are ridiculous." He took the towels and threw them in the trash. He didn't seem to care that his robe lay rumpled on the floor. "Come on."

Russell frowned, but Tristan grabbed his wrist and towed him through the apartment, down the hall, and through the bedroom into the master bathroom.

"Get in," Tristan said, twisting knobs on the wall. He nudged Russell in the direction of the shower alcove. Hot water already poured down from the multiple showerheads.

"This is the most absurd shower I've ever seen," he said, instead of talking about what he really wanted to say. Somehow, he didn't think Tristan was really up to the conversation Russell so desperately needed to have with him. Inside his head, the wild side of his mind howled and pushed at him, but for the first time he could remember since he and Tristan had pressed their cut and bleeding hands together, he was able to ignore it. He knew it was because of what they'd just done, and the energy they shared, but he didn't like being dependent on his friend for his sanity. *Especially when I'm not sure Tristan is entirely happy with this,* he thought, very privately.

"Yeah, yeah. Whatever. Take off your clothes," Tristan said.

Russell shucked his pants, then stepped into the spray. The hot water felt like heaven. When he'd washed up the night before, he'd been too tired to really enjoy Tristan's ridiculous shower. He let the water pound the tension out of his neck. "So, we're not going to talk about this?"

Tristan stepped in beside him. "What's to talk about?"

Russell snorted. "Oh, I don't know. The fact that I've moved in and no one knows we're together? And we very nearly fucked, and you're pushing me away?"

"I'm not pushing you anywhere except into my shower." Tristan soaped up his body. "I'm not in the habit of explaining myself to anyone." He gave Russell a sharp look. "And we're not together."

Russell shook his head. Somehow, he knew Tristan would react this way. He shoved the hurt down deep inside and slammed a lid on it. Tristan would not understand if he caught even a whiff of Russell's disappointment. However, that didn't mean he was going to let Tristan deny their bond. "You aren't serious."

Tristan frowned at him. The look wasn't particularly effective considering that he was also rinsing suds out of his hair. "I've never dated men."

Russell stared at his friend. "Tristan. We just got off together. We're connected." He waved a hand between them. "You can't deny the way our energy feeds off each other."

Tristan handed him the soap as if Russell hadn't spoken. "Wash up. We've got a busy day ahead of us."

"Tristan—" Russell began, but his friend cut him off.

"No. I can't talk about it. Not today." Tristan's face had closed down.

And here we go again. Dammit. Russell sighed. "Tristan, we have a mental bond. We've been in love with each other for the past twelve years. And you want to somehow pretend our relationship doesn't exist?"

Tristan turned his back. "The fewer people who know about us, the safer we'll be." He paused a moment, and Russell watched his back muscles tighten. "The safer *you'll* be."

Russell could feel Tristan's emotions roiling through their bond. "You realize I'm not going anywhere. It doesn't actually matter if we have sex or not. I'm here for good." He began to wash, watching as water sluiced down Tristan's absurdly ripped back. His friend's ass was insane. He imagined going to his knees and rimming him, and wondered what Tristan would do if he just took what he wanted so badly. He stepped closer. "So we might as well do it."

Tristan froze. "I don't want you dead, Russell."

That's what the problem is? Fear? Russell reached out and dumped the soap into the dish set in the wall alcove. "Tristan," he murmured, making sure he wasn't actually touching his lover anywhere. "I'm not your mother."

Tristan shuddered. "Fuck."

"And I'm certainly not your father." Russell put his hand on Tristan's shoulder. "I'm not going to die."

"You might," Tristan said quietly. "You can't tell the future."

"If I die, you'll probably be dead, too," Russell

pointed out. "So it doesn't matter if we do this." He slid his hand down Tristan's body until he could cup his friend's erection. Tristan groaned under his breath. Russell began to stroke him, touching Tristan exactly how he liked to touch himself. The weight of his friend's cock felt like home. The way his body shuddered against him felt like fucking paradise. "The only enemies we have are outsiders, Tris. The only leverage they have over us is each other, and that's only if we let them." He ran his thumb over the tip of his friend's shaft and stroked upwards. The water pounded down on them, hot enough to almost hurt, and he welcomed it. He felt as if he'd finally woken up after a decade's long sleep. "And I'm never leaving your side again." Stroke down. "You realize that, right?" Stroke up.

Tristan put his hands on the wall as his hips twitched forward, fucking his cock into Russell's fingers. "You can't be with me every hour of every day." His voice sounded rough.

Russell slid another hand around to play with Tristan's ass. "No? Are you sure about that?"

Tristan let his head hang down as his hips began to move faster. "It's impossible. I have meetings. I work eighteen-hour days. You need to shift into your beast, or you'll go insane." His breath hitched as Russell squeezed. "I have a Venezuelan cartel after me."

"Uh huh." Russell let his head drop over Tristan's shoulder so he could see what his hands were doing. His friend's cock was stiff, and the tip was red. Shiny. He stroked him faster as he slid a wet finger over Tristan's hole. "If I shift, you will be right there with me. If your enemies come after you, we will make them regret it. If you try to work eighteen-hour days, I'll physically drag you out of the office." He pressed his words into Tristan's body. He'd tattoo them into his lover's skin, if he could. As it was, he could feel Tristan trembling with desire. "Do you doubt me? I'm a man of my word. The moment I felt you inside my head a week ago, I knew it was time to come home. You can't get rid of me." Tristan widened his legs, and Russell's finger slid inside up to the first knuckle. Tristan's body was hot as hell, and he wanted inside so fucking bad. "I'm going to crawl inside you and stay forever."

"This is crazy." Tristan sounded desperate. "If we keep this up, and anyone finds out, you'll be a target."

As if something so minor could stop him. "I don't care," Russell said hotly. He knew how Tristan felt, and he understood his fear. But he'd just orgasmed a half hour ago, and his cock was hard enough to pound bricks all over again. This kind of desire couldn't be denied. "I can feel your emotions, Tristan," he said through clenched teeth. "You want me. You need me." He added another finger when Tristan didn't protest, stretching the tight muscles. "I need you."

Tristan let out a harsh breath. "So, what? I can feel your emotions, too. What we feel doesn't change reality. People will judge us for this. People will try to kill us for this."

"I don't give a damn. You have no intention of sending me away, and I wouldn't go even if you tried," Russell said, fitting the tip of his cock against Tristan's hole. They had no lube, and he knew that Tristan had never taken a cock up his ass before, but he couldn't seem to help himself. "Fuck. You feel good." He grabbed the soap and let suds slide down between their bodies as he thrust forward little by little.

Tristan leaned over, pressing back with his hips. "This is stupid." The soap fell to the floor as Russell groaned. Tristan breathed out, hands on the tile wall. "This is *impossible*." His voice cracked in the middle of his sentence.

Russell agreed, but he didn't stop. He couldn't stop. He'd go crazy if he tried to stop now, and he'd go crazy if he didn't keep going. Either way, they were doing this, and he could feel Tristan's acceptance in his bones. "Breathe," he said, hands curling over Tristan's hips. "Breathe, Tristan." He pushed forward gently, not even trying to get inside. Just feeling Tristan's amazing ass surrounding his erection was enough. He'd never get enough of Tristan. Never.

"Are you going to fuck me, or not?" Tristan asked raggedly.

Russell groaned, pushing a little harder. "I don't want to hurt you."

"You can feel my emotions," Tristan said, throwing the words back at Russell. "Do I feel like I'm in pain?"

"Yes. You do." Russell closed his teeth over Tristan's shoulder and bit down even as his free hand slid around Tristan's cock again. His friend felt like molten lava. Like lightning. Power flickered through them, just as wild and hot as earlier. There was pain, yes, but there was also an incendiary desperation in Tristan's energy. It drew Russell in and tore him to pieces. Now that he'd had a taste of it, he'd never be able to live without it. "I've never felt anything like this, Tristan," Russell said. The scent and heat of Tristan surrounded him. He'd never been so damned torn apart while also feeling perfectly at home.

Tristan fucked his cock into Russell's fist. "Neither have I." He had his hands clenched into fists, while water poured down around them like rain.

Russell moaned. Knowing that neither one of them had made love like this before did something to him. His hips jerked, and the tip of his erection slid inside, easing past the ring of muscles as Tristan shivered in his arms. "I'm never leaving your side again. You can't make me," he said roughly, hands stroking faster even as his cock pressed in further.

Tristan's shaft felt like fire in his hands. He'd be damned if he'd give this up after waiting so long for it. After waiting so long for *Tristan*. They were connected on a level that would make no sense to anyone else. They'd shared pain and distance and loneliness. They'd share death, and Russell would face anything gladly, if only he got to have Tristan as his lover. *Mate*, his beast whispered to him. He couldn't deny the truth of it.

Tristan didn't answer. He simply put his hands on the wall and opened his legs just enough so that Russell could sink in all the way.

"Fuck." Russell's control snapped, and suddenly he was fucking into Tristan, hard and rough. Tristan held strong, breathing in short gasps as Russell's thrusts pressed him into the tile. The heat of the water was nothing compared to what was happening between them.

"We're connected, Tristan." Russell punctuated his words with thrusts, as if fucking his friend would convince him of the truth. "And we always will be. Nothing can change that, no matter how much you try to deny it." The slick skin under his mouth tasted of water and soap and musk. He licked, then bit down again.

Tristan groaned. Russell's cock swelled. He changed the angle of his fucking, and Tristan threw back his head and cursed. Russell fucked him harder, feeling as if his body was melting into Tristan, as if they weren't two people at all. Their emotions tangled together: grief, regret, love, and heat bright enough to burn everything else away.

"Oh, God, Tristan. I'm so close," Russell growled as his balls drew up against his body.

"Do it," Tristan gasped, shaking beneath Russell's hands.

And suddenly Russell was coming, and Tristan's cock jerked, too, hot semen jetting out to mingle with the water pounding on the wall. He stopped breathing. He felt as if his entire body had turned itself inside out. The beast in him howled, then screamed, and for a moment he worried that he'd shift right here, and right now, but then the wildness transmuted into energy that roared down the bond they shared, opening up pathways he didn't know existed. Tristan's loneliness rushed through him, more than a match for his own. His cock jerked feebly as his orgasm slowly faded, and then his knees gave out.

They ended up on the floor in a heap.

A long time later, when the water finally began to cool, Tristan laughed, arms tangled with Russell's. "Well. I guess I was never really bi at all, was I?"

Russell shook his head. "No, Tristan," he said, voice barely loud enough to carry over the sound of water. It felt like they'd had sex in a rainstorm. It felt like he'd finally come home.

"My father would kill me for this." Tristan sounded exhausted all over again. "You realize that?"

"Your father is dead, and he can't hurt you anymore," Russell said quietly, wishing the old bastard had died years ago. *So much time wasted...* They could've been together for all this time, and instead, he'd had to run so they could both survive. "And even if he were still alive, he couldn't stop this. I'd have come home soon anyway."

Tristan sighed. "I should've shot him when he walked in on us kissing, all those years ago. I should've done a lot of things." He shifted his weight, as if he was going to stand up, but Russell wrapped his arms around his lover and buried his face in his neck.

"No. You would've ended up in jail, and I would probably be dead. We can't change the past. We can only change the future."

"Now you sound like my mother," Tristan murmured, stroking a finger down Russell's forearm.

Russell shivered. The cold water was finally getting to him. "And she would know." He pressed a kiss to Tristan's neck. "Come on." He stood up and hauled his lover to his feet. Tristan swayed. "Are you okay?" Russell asked, steadying him

"I'm fine." Tristan gave him a look that said Russell was being ridiculous. "I'm not fragile, as you know." He turned off the water, then shook his head. "My mother knew I loved you." He didn't look at Russell as he spoke. He grabbed two towels from the shelf just outside the shower and handed one to Russell. "She knew. Somehow."

"Did she tell you?" Russell asked, drying himself off roughly. His cock hung limp, but it wouldn't take much to wake it up again. Tristan stood nude in front of him, and Russell could see the scars on his torso from where his father had whipped him when he was a kid. He'd borne those scars for as long as Russell had known him. He wanted to kiss every single one of them. He wanted to take the pain away. He wanted Tristan to never feel alone again.

Tristan shrugged as he wrapped his towel around his waist. "She didn't have to say anything." He strode out of the shower alcove to the sink, and put his hands on the marble countertop, staring into the mirror. "I could sense it. One day I told her I knew you were still alive, and all she did was smile. She knew I loved you. I could feel it. She was okay with it."

Russell slowly walked up to Tristan. "Do you

know that she was the closest thing I've ever had to a mother?"

Tristan nodded. "I know," he whispered. "I always knew." He reached up and traced a line down the foggy mirror. "She was a good person trapped in an impossible life."

"We'll put her to rest, Tris. I promise," Russell said. He didn't mention the farce of a memorial service they had to get through, and he could see that Tristan knew he wasn't talking about that by the look on his face. "We'll find a way."

****

Four hours later, Russell stood in Tristan's kitchen in a brand-new black suit with a crisp white shirt, watching while his lover paced the room. Russell knew he looked like a bodyguard, and that's exactly what he wanted. His gaze roamed around, meeting the eyes of the two other men in Tristan's security detail before scoping the apartment again. The two men stood near the private elevator, inscrutable in matching black suits: Daniel Plakovitch and Jackson Maritozzi. He nodded to them, but they just scowled. Russell knew that Chesterfield must have told them he was calling the shots, and he knew they weren't happy about it. He didn't give a shit if that torqued them up. Tristan's safety was all that mattered, and with the cartel out for blood, Tristan needed more than a couple of guys to protect his back. His beast growled softly, urging him that he was all Tristan needed, but he resisted. Instinct wasn't enough this time. Not if he wanted to keep Tristan alive.

"I'm tired of waiting," Tristan said suddenly.

"The car will be here in ten minutes," Russell told him.

Tristan stopped pacing and glared at him. "My mother didn't want this stupid bullshit service. We both know it. Even if it's small and private, it's still going to be too much. There'll be too much ass-licking and not enough genuine mourning." He turned his head to look at the small, elaborately decorative urn resting on the countertop. It was empty. It would remain empty. Julia Marik's ashes currently resided in a nondescript box tucked away in Tristan's dresser. "She'd hate that thing, and I wouldn't blame her."

"She'd understand," Russell said. "It's just for show." That urn was for good of the company and to let their enemies know that Tristan Marik was still alive, and intended on staying that way. That urn was nothing more than advertising.

"She hated this shit, Russell, and you know it," Tristan disagreed. He ran his hands through his hair, mussing the dark strands. "Her entire life was on display, and now so is her death. It's not right."

Russell watched Dan and Jackson while Tristan spoke. Neither man showed any emotion, but he could sense a weird kind of echo through Tristan. Dan was professional: alert and detached. Jackson was not. He eyed the man, but his outward appearance didn't match the anger inside. He made a mental note to keep an eye on the guy. Tristan's life was on the line, and he hadn't had time to comb through Monolith's internal security personnel files as thoroughly as he'd like.

"Do you hear me?" Tristan asked, stopping directly in front of Russell. His eyes snapped with irritation.

"Nothing can hurt her anymore," Russell said quietly. He looked at Tristan steadily, willing his lover to understand that he wouldn't let anything happen to him. That he understood he was hurting. "You know she'd never blame you for doing what you have to do."

Tristan sighed noisily. "Yeah, yeah. Doesn't

mean I'm happy about this."

Russell wished he could reach out and hug him, but Tristan had talked him into keeping their true relationship under wraps. He could feel his beast inside, itching to get out and destroy anyone who dared hurt Tristan, and he knew it was partly because he wanted everyone to know that Tristan was *his*.

He inhaled, long and slow, leashing his beast with iron self-control. He had no idea where this possessive streak came from, but he didn't have the energy to fight it, *and* keep his shifting under control. Tristan was *his*, and they both knew it. It didn't matter who else knew. When his earpiece beeped, he nodded at Dan and Jackson. It was time to go.

"Come on," he said, reaching for the urn. The last thing he was going to do was make Tristan carry it. He tucked it under his arm. "Let's get this show on the road." The bodyguards headed for the elevator, but Russell waited for Tristan to step ahead of him before following.

"We'll put her to rest the right way," Tristan said quietly, tapping a finger on the urn. "Later. When everyone stops watching."

Russell nodded. "We will."

Tristan's expression softened for a moment, and then he pivoted and headed for the lift. Russell followed him, wishing Tristan's life weren't so damned complicated.

Chapter Six

Tristan sat in his limo, wishing he were someone different. Someone invisible. Someone whose life hadn't been filled with death and blood and a father who thought nothing of screwing around with thousands of people's lives. He stared moodily out the window as the vehicle slowly drove uptown to Trinity Mausoleum. He didn't want to even pretend to lay his mother to rest there, but he had no choice. He had to make it look good. The old bastard's ashes could rot in hell for all he cared, but of course his father's remains would be interred in the small crypt set aside for the Marik family, along with his mother's empty urn. The best he could do to get through this was to pretend that this service was for just for his mother.

"Heads up," Russell murmured from across the seat.

Tristan sighed, shifting his weight. His security guy, Dan, was in the front seat with his driver, and Jackson sat next to him. He could feel the weight of the man's rage pressing in on him. He rubbed his temples with his fingers, wishing Jackson would give it a rest. He couldn't help it that his father was dead. Hell, he was *happy* the old man was dead. Jackson blamed him.

God help me if he ever finds out that I pulled the trigger…

"Jackson, when we stop, you take point," Russell said, dark eyes cold as he looked at Tristan's bodyguard.

Tristan knew Russell could feel Jackson's ire through their bond, and that helped. At least Russell knew to be wary. If Tristan had had his way, he would have had someone else assigned to this detail, but they'd run out of time to reorganize the service. He glanced at Jackson, not missing the pursed lips and glare. He sighed, then caught Russell's gaze and nodded. Russell tilted his head a fraction, and Tristan shook his head minutely. Russell looked away.

He knows we can't do anything about it now, Tristan mused, fidgeting his thumb over his palm. He didn't think the man would betray him, but he'd been wrong before. He just had to hope Dan and Russell could handle anything unexpected.

Jackson gave Russell a distrustful look, but he looked away when Russell just stared at him, brown eyes cold and hard. Tristan smiled internally. Russell could intimidate anyone. He was big and muscular, and on top of that, he carried an edge of wildness that people instinctively shied away from.

Delicious, Tristan thought, remembering the way Russell had grunted as he fucked him into the wall in the shower. Tristan liked that hint of brutality, but he understood how frightening others found it. Jackson looked down, then out of the window, as if merely glancing around instead of avoiding Russell's stare. Tristan smirked. Russell was *his*. All of that power and menace belonged to him, and he had the bruises to prove it.

"Almost there," Dan said, twisting around from the front seat to let them know.

"Thanks," Tristan said quietly, still watching Jackson. He suspected his father had used Jackson to spy on him, and if so, the man's days as his bodyguard were numbered. He lifted an eyebrow at Russell, and his lover's lips quirked. Russell knew Jackson couldn't be trusted. *At least this bond is good for something other than sex.*

When the car halted, Tristan looked out the window. They'd pulled directly onto the grounds through the gates, and then stopped near the set of stone steps that led up to the crypt. He frowned. A small cluster of people his father had done business with waited outside, like a flock of vultures roosting on a decayed house, only this time the house was his family. The house was him and Russell, and the last thing he wanted to do was open the door and walk inside. He'd invited the absolute minimum of people that he could, but it still felt like too many for a private service. Tristan gritted his teeth, briefly wondering how long it would take for him to develop an ulcer. *Probably not long at this rate.*

Beyond the vultures, the group of employees who'd decided to attend was small, thank fuck. He hadn't invited any family members, mostly because he had none. His mother had been an only child, and her parents were long dead. *There's only me and Russell left,* he thought, not sure if he should be grateful or sad that no one really even knew that Russell was his boyfriend.

"Time to roll," Russell said, tapping his earpiece and tugging Tristan out of his pointless rumination. Tristan knew Russell was receiving reports from the larger security detail. He also knew that men had searched the surrounding buildings, and everyone who wanted to attend the service had to give up their cell phones and any weapons, but he couldn't trust anyone right now. Security was tight, but he knew as well as Russell did that none of these precautions would stop the cartel if they wanted to make a move. And he knew that it was likely that they would. And it was also just as likely that he couldn't rely on his own security force, so God only knew how many guns were in the cluster of people waiting to watch him put his grief on display.

I wonder if I'm going to die today, he mused, somewhat irritated by his grim train of thought. He ought to be happy: his father was finally dead and Russell was home, but instead, anxiety prowled through his bones like an unwelcome visitor. He expected a catastrophe, because that's how most of the rest of his life had gone. It was absurd to think it would be any different now that his parents were dead.

Jackson got out of the car, standing in front of the door for a moment until Dan joined him. Russell put a hand on Tristan's knee. "Keep alert. Something is going to go wrong." He glanced around. "I don't trust Chesterfield's men."

Doesn't something always go wrong? Tristan thought sardonically, but he nodded his agreement anyway, not surprised that Russell was on the same page as he was. "Of course." He gathered his mother's fake urn, tucking it into the crook of his arm. "This is a circus." His gaze narrowed as he peered out of the open door. "Vultures. Look at them circling." He glared at the clot of people. Most of them wore black as if to show respect, but he knew they were simply waiting to peck at his remains.

"I know." Russell's voice was sad.

"No reason for *you* to be sad." Tristan shook his head, then climbed out of the car when Dan gave him the all-clear signal. Russell followed, keeping close to Tristan's back. There was no way anyone was getting through him, and though the idea of Russell putting himself in harm's way terrified Tristan, it also soothed him. He wasn't alone. He'd never be alone again, thank God.

"This way, Mr. Marik," the funeral director said, appearing at his side as if teleported there. His white hair and thin frame didn't match his deep voice. "As requested by your security chief, everyone in attendance has been searched and gone through metal detectors. There will be no need to worry about your safety while here, I assure you, sir."

Tristan nodded to him, but didn't speak. There was nothing to say, after all. He glanced around as he climbed the stairs, glad he hadn't made the ceremony public. The quiet murmur of voices washed over him, but it was the emotions that crashed down and truly hurt, dwarfing everything else. He held back a flinch as his control slipped for a moment. If Russell's warm, strong presence hadn't been directly behind him, he would've been crushed by it all. He gritted his teeth and climbed to the top of the steps, then paused.

"Here, sir," the director said, gesturing to Tristan to place the urn on a small table in front of the Marik family crypt. It felt disturbingly final. For a moment, Tristan had to stop and just breathe. His mother's ashes weren't even here, for Christ's sake. Grief pushed up through his walls, and he knew Russell could sense it, too. He looked blindly around at the flowering shrubs and the absurd mass of floral arrangements someone had organized and fought off a wave of anger. He *hated* this. Hated it.

"Steady," Russell murmured, and his voice gave Tristan the strength to carry on.

Tristan placed the urn on the table, bitterly noting that someone had put his father's larger, more elaborate urn there as well. "I didn't order this," he bit out. He'd thought it would be inside the crypt. He'd *hoped* the damned thing would be inside the crypt.

The funeral director's face froze. "I'm sorry. I was told that the will stipulated—"

Tristan raised his arm, cutting the man off. "Of course it did." He'd forgotten about that. The lawyers had read the will the day before Russell arrived. The only surprise in it was that Tristan had inherited everything with no strings attached. He'd been sure his father would make him jump through hoops, but perhaps the old bastard hadn't expected to die so soon. He smiled grimly as he arranged his mother's urn in front of his father's, and then stepped back. As in life, his father's urn dwarfed the one Tristan had to pretend was for his mother, and a surge of rage shot though him. He wished he could kill the old man all over again for his crimes, this time more slowly and painfully. He ignored the chairs placed in front of the small table. He'd be damned if he was going to sit down for this.

"Would you like to say a few words?" the funeral director asked him.

Tristan stared at the man. "Mr. Philips, right?"

"Yes, Mr. Marik." The man nodded. "I'm so very sorry for your loss."

Useless words, Tristan thought bitterly. "Fine." He strode forward, sensing swelling emotions as he stood next to the table. Russell's solid strength helped shore up his mental walls, and he shut everything down until he could barely feel anything at all. "My mother was a strong, kind, and intelligent woman. Not many people knew her, and fewer people knew how much she suffered in her life." He took a deep breath, looking out over the few attendees. He saw his assistant, Meredith, standing with one of the ground floor receptionists, Marlie. Even his assistant had no idea how abusive his father had been, and she'd witnessed the old man screaming at Tristan more than once. Poor woman. He wouldn't be surprised if she needed therapy from her time at Monolith. He'd be even less surprised if she didn't quit in the next month once she realized that she was free.

Tristan looked out over the courtyard and made a decision. He was done hiding the abuse. "My father abused my mother every day of their lives together. I'm glad he's dead, and I'm glad she had a hand in sending him to hell, where he belongs."

Tristan smiled grimly as Marlie's shock pushed at him. "My mother saved my life more than once. I'm only sorry I was too late to save hers." With that, he stepped away. There was too much death here for him to want to linger, and he had nothing to say to anyone who came hoping to see a spectacle. His gaze met Russell's, and he recognized approval in his friend's face. He nodded, then stood in front of the chairs, still not sitting. He'd never be able to stand up again if he sat now.

The funeral director waited a moment, but when no one else came forward, he smoothly took over, saying a few pointless words of sympathy, and then reading a short prayer. Tristan stood with his hands clenched into fists, emotions and power locked down, wishing he was back in his penthouse. Wishing he was back in the shower with Russell, the way they had been this morning, with Russell fucking inside him. He'd felt alive. He'd felt loved. Right now, he felt neither of those things. He thought he'd feel like less of a man after taking another man's cock inside his body, but instead he'd felt more real than he'd felt before in his life. Russell saw who he truly was. Russell was the only one who did. And so Tristan stared straight ahead, waiting for this farce of a service to end.

When a low, animalistic growl rolled through the courtyard, he snapped his head around, thinking Russell had shifted. But no, Russell stood next to him, frowning. "Did you hear that?"

His lover slashed his hand out, and Tristan fell silent. The funeral director droned on, and no one else seemed to notice, but then he heard it again. *That sounds like a wolf,* he thought, confused. Russell was right next to him, and his mouth was closed. There were no wolves in New York City. That meant either someone was messing with him by blasting the sound from somewhere outside the grounds of the mausoleum, or there was—

"Down!" Russell tackled him, knocking over three chairs. Tristan landed on his back, all the wind knocked out of him. His power crashed against the mental walls he'd erected, and then blasted out. Fury and determination washed through him, and he twisted around, trying to see beyond Russell's solid body.

"Fuck," Russell bit out, rolling off Tristan. He'd pulled his weapon, but the people attending had gone insane, hurling themselves over the chairs. There was no clear shot, and no one to shoot at.

Tristan caught sight of Meredith's frightened face as she fell, and then the wolves came.

****

Russell's heart pounded a thousand times a second, or at least that's what it felt like as he watched a huge goddamn wolf pack tear through the chairs and fallen people as they tried to get to him and Tristan. And these were no ordinary wolves, oh no. They were huge, and they were intent on killing, and that meant that his fucking father's experiments with his blood had somehow born evil fruit. *This must be the bio-pharmaceutical venture Tris couldn't find out about*, he thought, even as rage welled up inside of him like a forest fire, crackling and violent. His beast took that rage and used it to try to burst free. Russell ruthlessly muzzled his emotions. If he shifted now, he wouldn't be able to think, and Tristan needed him functional. Tristan rolled into a crouch, and Russell thanked God that his mate wasn't easily rattled. *They created shifters*, he thought, imagining the money to be had with such a product. No wonder Tristan's father got in bed with a cartel.

"What the fuck?" Tristan asked, face tight with strain as his gaze darted across the courtyard.

"Stay down," Russell snarled, still trying to figure

87

out how the hell to get out of this sudden disaster. He spun around, instinct screaming at him to get Tristan away, but they were surrounded. Jackson stood over Dan, weapon pointed at his head. He smiled, and Russell cursed under his breath. He'd *known* the guy couldn't be trusted, but he'd had no time to set up a replacement.

I should've dismissed him, he thought, but before he could say a word let alone do anything, Jackson shot Dan in the head. He looked right at Russell, eyes triumphant, and then the man shifted from human to wolf and joined the pack surrounding him and Tristan. The few humans left were cowering on the ground. "Fucking hell," he muttered, wondering if he'd have time to change shape before they attacked. Something inside told him that there was no way he'd be able to fight these wolves unless he shifted into something bigger than they were. Something much worse.

"They're here to kill us, Russell," Tristan said. "I don't know how or why, but they're hunting together. They have an alpha, and he's directing them, just the way a pack would in the wild." Tristan's voice was low and steady, and Russell felt a wave of energy move through him via their bond. The emotions he sensed were filtered through Tristan's mind, and he bared his teeth. These wolves were not exactly wild animals. They were like him. They were shifters. His mother had told him that the only way for that to happen was to be born to one of the few, vanishing bloodlines that carried the shifter gene, which meant that these came from his father's experimental gene therapy. His father had stolen his blood and created monsters with it for money, damn him to hell.

"Jesus Christ," Russell bit out. "My fucking father—"

"And mine," Tristan interrupted, Glock in hand.

"Don't forget about him. The two of them must have kept working on that damned therapy even after you'd gone. This is the shit I couldn't track down, Russell. The amount of money he made from it was ridiculous." He made a sound in the back of his throat. "You realize, I wouldn't be surprised if my father killed yours. He wouldn't have wanted to share in the profits. I know you were told it was an aneurysm, but I no longer believe it." He maneuvered until he was at Russell's back.

"Aneurysm or murder, it doesn't matter now," Russell said tightly. "The cartel wants revenge on you for shutting it down." The snarling wolves had mauled some of the people in the memorial service's audience, and dimly, Russell recognized the broken body lying near the steps as one of Tristan's first floor receptionists.

"Dan's dead. We're boxed in," Tristan said, pointing out the obvious.

"So is one of your receptionists. I think your assistant is okay, though." Russell felt his control shredding. There was only one form he knew that would be able to handle this situation, but he'd never told Tristan about it. Hell, he'd only ever shifted into it once, and it had scared the living shit out of him when he had. "Whatever happens, don't freak out, Tristan," he said grimly, already preparing himself for the change. *Thank fuck the service was so small. We might just be able to keep this under wraps, if we're very, very careful.*

"Russell?" Tristan looked wary.

Russell shook his head at his lover. There was nothing he could do. He'd get Tristan out of this if it killed him. His beast howled his frustration into his mind, and Russell knew he didn't have much time before instinct took over. His mate was in danger, and he had to act.

"Don't, Russell," Tristan said, voice like iron.

"Whatever you're thinking, you don't have to do it. No one knows about you. I don't want anyone to know."

"We're surrounded. We're going to die. The risk is worth it." Russell felt Tristan's fear deep in his bones, but it didn't matter. He had to do this if they wanted to live. "Your life is worth it," he said grimly, and he handed Tristan his weapon. Two guns were better than one, and now at least Tristan could shoot anyone who attacked him while Russell changed.

"No—" Tristan said, but Russell had already let go of the chains around his beast, and the creature surged to the front of his consciousness, wild and furious, and not a moment too soon. The wolves surrounding them had clearly decided that enough was enough. The alpha wolf, as big as a fucking bear, leaped.

Tristan yelled, shooting it at point blank range, but it didn't even slow the bastard down. Russell felt his skin ignite, and the next thing he knew, his scales scraped the granite pavers, cracking several as he turned and breathed fire into the left flank of wolves. They ignited and died, although the wolf leading the charge swerved at the last moment, choosing to run away.

The few remaining people screamed, fleeing the grounds as he turned his head and swept the wolves on their right with his barbed tail. They howled and snarled and attacked, but they had no defense against *him*. They might be wolves, but he was a living nightmare.

"Jesus," Tristan said, face white as he stared up at Russell's new form. Deep green scales swirled with metallic black reflected in his eyes.

Russell had lost the ability to speak with his shift, but luckily, Tristan wasn't stupid. After a moment's hesitation, he simply holstered his weapon and pocketed the other, and then he climbed up onto Russell's back, hooking his legs over the spines at the base of his neck.

Inside Russell's mind, his beast howled in satisfaction. *Mate,* he thought, satisfied. As before when he'd shifted in Tristan's company, he retained enough humanity to marvel at the feeling. He could *think,* but more importantly, he could plan. He needed to get them out of here, but how to do it without causing a massive panic?

"I'm secure," Tristan said, leaning down. He slid his hands over Russell's scales. "Don't worry about me. Don't worry about anyone seeing you. I suddenly have enough power to blank the vision of everyone in this entire city." He laughed, and there was an edge of hysteria to the sound. "Imagine that."

Russell knew that Tristan's power was magnified with him in this form, because he could *feel* it, pulsing in his head. Tristan's energy was as big as Russell's physical form, and that meant he could probably wipe out a thousand people with a single thought, not that he would.

I'm just going to be grateful about this gift, and not think too hard about it, he thought as he turned his great head and carefully breathed more fire, this time catching the table with the urns. Unlike ordinary flame, his burned hotter than normal. The urns exploded and instantly vaporized, along with another cluster of wolves. Gunfire splattered against his hide, and he whirled around again. Men on the roof outside the security perimeter were firing at them, and he couldn't tell if they were Tristan's people or the cartel's.

"Ignore them!" Tristan yelled. "Get us the fuck out of here."

Russell wondered if Tristan really knew what he was asking for, but another round of gunfire made the point moot. In this form, he was bulletproof, but Tristan wasn't. He growled, and long tendrils of flame leaked out of his snout as he opened his wings. He scraped the edge of the mausoleum. Wolves leaped up onto him, trying to get to Tristan, but they couldn't grip his hide and slid down, snarling and snapping. Russell ignored them to breathe a wall of flame at the sky, and then he leaped.

Chapter Seven

Tristan didn't know how he managed it, but somehow, he flung out his power in a wide swath through the city once Russell clawed his way into the air. His ability to influence emotion spun out like a thin weave of energy—not enough to drain him, but enough to dissuade anyone who might see them from looking up, and anyone already looking up from registering what they saw. He couldn't keep this up for long, and he wasn't sure if he was doing enough to disguise their flight, but he had to try. Exhaustion slid through him the harder he pushed out his power, and if he hadn't been literally riding on top of Russell, he'd never have been able to do even this much. Their bond amplified everything, but there were limits. He felt a glimmer of worry seep through their bond from his lover, and he grimaced.

He sent a wordless reassurance to Russell and closed his eyes. It was easier if he couldn't see. Even as he dug his fingers into Russell's warm scales, his mind whispered down the length and breadth of the energy wave: *look away, look away.* Buildings scrolled by like smears of concrete smashed on his vision, and he could only hang on and breathe and thank God none of the bullets flying through the courtyard had caught him. If he'd been injured, they would never have escaped.

Beneath his grip, Russell beat huge wings, dark as nightfall. They lurched with heart-stopping drops, and Tristan worried they wouldn't stay aloft. Russell was huge and angry and impossible, but his flight was still bound by the laws of physics. Tristan leaned down, pressing his forehead onto the warm scales beneath him until Russell found a thermal above the buildings. Suddenly, they glided as smoothly as if they were swimming along some sedate current and Tristan breathed a sigh of relief.

Open your eyes, he told himself. The higher up they were, the fewer minds he had to try to influence, so he eased back. For all that they were in Manhattan, few people ever simply looked up. He opened his eyes and drew his power back a bit, relieved as he looked over Russell's spines. Or at least, he had been relieved until he abruptly realized there was nothing between them and the ground but trust. When he'd first scrambled up onto Russell's neck, he'd been desperate, and he'd mistakenly thought flying would feel the same as a helicopter, but he'd thought wrong.

It feels like fucking jumping into thin air, he thought, skin prickling with energy. He gripped the scales beneath him, and somehow kept up a whisper of *look away*, but then they dropped lower and he had to push harder again. He sensed rather than saw people staring up at them, and he wondered how long it would be before he collapsed. He'd skirted the edges of what was possible before, and he'd paid for it the next day, but he'd do whatever he had to if it meant protecting Russell.

I'm spreading myself too thin, he worried, but the next thing he knew, they were landing on the roof of Monolith Tower. The entire journey had taken a few minutes, maybe less. Before Tristan could speak, Russell tipped him down, sending him sliding down the scales along his shoulder. Tristan landed on his feet, a miracle in itself, and then Russell tucked his wings away as delicately as an origami bird folding in on itself. Suddenly, Tristan was standing on his rooftop courtyard staring at Russell crouched on the marble pavers, head down. Nude.

Tristan blinked as his power rushed back at him in a strong, hot wave. The energy he'd put out hadn't dissipated, but it was no longer needed, and it was a hell of a thing to pull it all back in and close it down, but he gritted his teeth and did it. He leaned over, hands on his knees, fighting for air. He felt a bit like he'd just swallowed a volcano. When he finally looked up, Russell's gaze met his. A glimmer of the beast lingered in Russell's eyes, wild and angry.

Well, shit. Tristan went from shock to lust in a heartbeat. "Russell." He staggered forward, grabbing his lover by the shoulders. Russell's skin was hot as hell. *And why wouldn't it be?* Tristan wondered, half-hysterically. "You're a dragon. My God."

"Only sometimes," Russell said, standing up, and Tristan pulled him into a kiss, not caring that he wasn't even trying to be gentle. Fuck gentle. Russell could handle his strength.

Russell can handle anything, Tristan thought wildly. "We're alive," he growled against Russell's mouth. He bit down into his lover's lower lip because he was worried that they'd both fly off the building if he didn't do something to ground them here.

"You think I'd let you die?" Russell asked, sounding angry. His hands were on Tristan's arms. "I'd do anything to keep you alive, Tristan, even expose all of our secrets. Luckily, very few people actually saw us, and most of them already know about shifting. The rest, you can handle."

"I realize that." Tristan shook his head, trying to gather the shreds of his control. "I just wasn't expecting *this.*" He waved a hand at Russell. "You're, you're…" he stuttered, and then he gave up, kissing Russell again. He tasted of fire and ash and *home.*

Russell groaned, sinking his hands into Tristan's hair. "Yeah, I know," he said roughly, letting Tristan scrape his teeth along his jaw. "I *know,* Tris."

Tristan pulled back abruptly and began tearing at his suit. He needed to feel Russell's skin against his. His mind felt so electric he thought he might die, but at least Russell was right there with him—powerful, angry, and hot as hell. "I can't even—" he tried to say, but then he gave up. He couldn't speak right now. He couldn't do anything so trite as piece together *words* into *sentences.* He got his jacket off and threw it to the ground, then started in on the buttons of his shirt. He needed to be naked, right the fuck now.

Growling, Russell moved in, ripping at Tristan's clothes. His tie went flying, and then Russell rent the fabric of his shirt into tatters. "I need to fuck you. Can I fuck you?"

"No." Tristan laughed, and then he shook his head. "No, I'm going to fuck *you,* Russell."

Russell stared at him, eyes burning, and then he nodded. He stripped Tristan's pants and shoes off with no finesse. Tristan's skin burned, but he didn't care.

"No one will bother us up here?" Russell asked, looking up the length of Tristan's body. He leaned in, pressing lips to his thighs.

Tristan shivered, but he wasn't cold. He was burning up, as if a fever had taken hold of him. He felt like screaming. He felt like fucking until neither of them remembered who they were or why they'd waited so long.

"There had better not be anyone here," he ground out, but even as he spoke, he sent his power out in a huge wave throughout the entire tower. They were on his private roof courtyard, but Russell was right. He didn't want visitors—not *any* kind. He found a few men and his security chief in their office on the third floor and knocked them into unconsciousness, and not gently. Chesterfield hadn't any clue that Jackson was a traitor, but he also hadn't caught the man, and because of that, Tristan had almost fucking died. It served the man right to spend the rest of the day on the floor of his office. The remainder of the building was empty, because Tristan had locked it down for the day, against many protests. No one was inside, not renters, not employees. Not one soul.

"All set?" Russell asked, face rigidly controlled. He'd stood up, and was pressed up against Tristan's body. To Tristan, his lover felt as though he'd just stepped out of a sauna: hot skin, hard cock, tight fingers on Tristan's biceps.

Tristan nodded, staring into Russell's wild dragon eyes. Not all of the beast had gone back into Russell's mind, and he liked it. He liked seeing that fire in there. "Everyone is unconscious."

Russell's expression tightened even more. "What if the cartel comes?"

"Then we will burn this fucking building to the ground with them inside," Tristan said, knowing he sounded absolutely crazy. He didn't give a flying fuck.

Instead of freaking, Russell nodded as if what he'd said made perfect sense, his eyes going dark and sure. "Then, fuck me, Tristan. I've been waiting long enough. I've been waiting for twelve fucking years."

Tristan's cock twitched, and pre-cum slid from the slit on top. His hips jerked, rubbing his slick all over Russell's groin. "Jesus Christ," he said, clenching his teeth. He grabbed Russell's wrist and dragged him to one of the chaises set near the small pool. "Down."

Russell fell onto his back. The fact that he had enough power over Russell, a fucking *dragon*, to push him down onto his back only revved Tristan up higher. He looked around, nearly frantic with need, then pulled the tray of condiments set on the glass table near the chaise closer. Salt and sugar scattered as he grabbed the bottle of olive oil left over from some lunch he'd had last week. He hadn't let anyone in to clean up after him after all hell had broken loose in his life, and now he was glad he'd insisted on privacy. He drizzled a generous amount of the oil over his hand, then cupped himself, oiling his cock while Russell watched with greedy eyes.

"This is for you," he said, not recognizing his own voice. He sounded like a man who'd gone through hell and come back changed. *And is that entirely wrong?* a small voice at the back of his mind asked.

"God, Tristan," Russell said, staring at Tristan's hand. "You have no idea how badly I want you." He gripped his own erection, squeezing until Tristan wondered how he stood the pain. "Stop teasing. I don't have the patience for it."

"Is this what you want?" Tristan got on his knees on the chaise, pushing Russell's thighs wide. His heavy balls lolled, then drew up tight when Tristan touched a finger to Russell's cock. He felt hot and huge, and Tristan remembered well how it had felt inside his body. "You want me?" He leaned down. He didn't have it in him to go slow right now. Russell's cock lay thick and hard along his groin, so Tristan slicked some of the oil on him, too.

Russell shuddered as he grabbed Tristan's hips hard enough to hurt. His fingertips burned as if he hadn't entirely put out the fire that was his dragon's form. "Yes," he hissed pulling Tristan down. "Come on."

Tristan gripped himself and lined up. "I don't want to hurt you."

Russell snorted. "I can change my body's shape at will, Tristan. You're not going to hurt me." He leaned in and bit Tristan's lip. "Come on. Put your cock in my body. You're not afraid of a little fire, are you?"

The thought of Russell shifting his shape nearly sent Tristan over the edge before they'd even begun. *All that power, and he's begging for me.* And then the thought of Russell's dragon breathing fire and fury down on their enemies pushed him even closer to the edge. "I'm not going to be able to go slow," he said through clenched teeth as he pressed the tip of his erection to Russell's hole.

"I'm a dragon, not a fragile flower," Russell said, opening up to Tristan as if this was exactly where they were meant to be. He cupped Tristan's ass and *pulled.*

"Oh my God," Tristan said as Russell's heat enveloped his cock. "Oh my fucking God."

Russell groaned, wrapping his legs around Tristan's torso. "Fuck me. Do it hard."

Tristan's hips snapped forward so roughly, Russell grunted. Tristan put his hands on Russell's shoulders as he pulled out, then thrust back in. There was nothing gentle about what he did. And if he'd had any doubt, Russell's legs and arms dragging him closer pushed it away.

"Come *on*, Tristan," Russell said, sounding like he was on the verge of a heart attack. He looked up at Tristan, power swirling in his eyes. His beast was in there, too: the wolf and the hawk and the dragon. He wasn't anything tame, and he never would be.

He doesn't have to be tame. He just has to be mine. Tristan bared his teeth and thrust in again, and then again, harder each time until the pressure of their bodies hitting each other pushed the chaise along the pavers. Sweat slid down Tristan's shoulders, then along the small of his back. He hissed as Russell's body heated his, and everything felt like fire and flame and pleasure. He cried out, needing to orgasm, but he couldn't quite get there.

"Let go, Tristan," Russell gasped. His fingers dug

into Tristan's hips hard enough to bruise. "Let go."

Tristan wasn't sure what Russell meant for a moment, and then suddenly he did. He lowered his mental barriers, and his mind swept out to meet the impossible heat of Russell's beast. Their energy fought for a split second and then merged. Russell groaned as Tristan bit down on his shoulder. The salty-hot tang of Russell's blood in his mouth sent Tristan over, and they both screamed as pleasure pushed through them like an eruption. Tristan smelled ash and smoke, and Russell's eyes were flaming and he was flying, and then their climax gripped them and he couldn't think anymore, so he just … let go.

A long time later, Tristan inhaled shakily. They were glued together with sweat and cum and exhaustion.

"You're okay," Russell said gently, hands stroking down Tristan's back. Their sweat had dried even though they lay directly in the heat of the afternoon sun. Russell was hotter than mere sunlight, after all.

"Yeah," Tristan said, almost not recognizing his voice. "I'm okay." He let himself slide sideways, tucking their bodies together on a chaise that was really too small for two grown men, let alone grown men their size. "I don't think many people saw you change. The wolves had already torn through the crowd."

"I know some of them saw," Russell said tiredly. "But hopefully not enough to start an investigation. I'd prefer it if the regular human world remained in the dark, much as it always has."

Tristan grimaced. "I'm sorry. I could never have predicted … *that*."

After a moment, Russell sighed. "I'm not. I'd do it over again in a heartbeat to keep you safe."

Tristan pushed up, staring down at Russell's face. "I'd hide it forever to keep *you* safe."

Russell stared at him, eyes faded back to almost ordinary brown. A hint of his beast lingered, and Tristan had a feeling it always would. He wasn't human anymore, after all. He'd never really been fully human. *And neither am I, now*, he realized.

"Are you going to try to keep *us* a secret, though?" Russell asked. "If so, we've got a problem."

Tristan stopped breathing. The thought of coming out, and letting everyone know how much Russell meant to him—

Russell's expression shut down. "Never mind. I can see it on your face." He rolled off the chaise and stood up, not seeming to care about the drying spunk flaking off of his abdomen. He moved as if he hadn't just had another man's cock up his ass. He looked strong. He looked *angry*.

Damn it. Tristan stood up, too, not surprised that his legs were shaky. "It's not that I'm ashamed of you—"

Russell cut him off with a harsh snort. "Please." He turned his back. "Don't even try that shit with me, Tris."

Tristan strode around and grabbed Russell's arms. "I'm *not* ashamed!" He wished he could shake sense into his lover. "I'm fucking scared to death that someone will see how much you mean to me and take you away."

Russell blinked. "Are you kidding me?" He shrugged off Tristan's grip and ran a hand over his face. "Tristan, I would out myself as a shifter to the entire world to keep you safe and alive." He flung out an arm. "So I don't think it really matters all that much how obvious it is that you love me back, and not the way a friend would love me. You're my lover, Tristan. My *mate*." His eyes flared with anger as he nearly spat out the words. "We're supposed to be partners, and I want the world to know it."

Tristan took a step back, half expecting smoke to come out of Russell's mouth. "Mate?" he whispered, even as his heart gave a sick thud against his ribcage.

Russell rolled his eyes. "You can't be that delusional, Tristan." He thrust out a hand, palm up. The silvery scar that showed where they'd sworn a blood oath to each other as stupid, clueless teens shone in the sunlight. "We're fucking bonded. I can feel your emotions. I've been able to feel them for years, even from half a world away. This isn't news to you, so don't try to deny it."

Tristan swallowed. He could feel Russell's emotions, too, loud and clear. And he knew the man loved him. He knew he loved Russell. *But I'm terrified, and not afraid to admit it.*

Russell growled.

"I don't know how we can go public without triggering a disaster," Tristan said. If people found out, they'd try to take Russell away. After all, wasn't that what his father had done? His throat ached, as if he were trying to keep down some giant worm lodged in his chest and the damned thing was fighting to get out. "And I can't lose you."

"Tristan," Russell said quietly, moving forward and grabbing Tristan's shoulders. "It's too late. It's way too fucking late to put the dragon back in the box."

Chapter Eight

Russell watched Tristan shower. He'd already washed, but he'd be damned if he'd give Tristan privacy, especially not after Tristan's idiotic denial of their bond. *Maybe not ever.*

"I can feel you watching me," Tristan said, back turned. Suds slid down his beautifully muscular back.

Idly, Russell wondered what it would be like if Tristan had been a woman. Would he still feel this frantic anger and lust and love all mixed up for him? Or would he feel gentler? More patient? As it was, he wanted to shake Tristan until all of his fears fell out of him, and then he wanted to stomp the damned things into fragments. *If only emotions were objects, life would be so much simpler,* he mused.

"You don't have to watch over me in the bathroom," Tristan said, washing his hair now. "No one is going to come for me in here. There's only one way into the bathroom. Hell, there's only one way into the apartment, not counting the roof." He twisted, rinsing as he placed the shampoo bottle back on the shelf. "I'm safe."

"I don't give a shit," Russell said, crossing his arms. "It's not about being safe anymore. It's about not letting you out of my sight." He'd put on his last pair of jeans, but hadn't bothered with a shirt. And he'd bet twenty bucks that he was going to have to shift and ruin these pants within the next twenty-four hours.

Tristan turned the water off. "You're being stubborn." He ran a hand down his face, sluicing water off his skin. "And you know it."

Russell lifted a shoulder. He was much more interested in watching Tristan bathe than he was in arguing about something he'd already decided to do.

"Doesn't cost me anything to be stubborn."

"You're impossible." Tristan's green eyes glittered as he dried off. Russell could feel the power banked behind his lover's control, and it fed his beast's energy.

"If you die, I die. If you live, I'll be right by your side. I don't care what people think," Russell finally said when he sensed Tristan wasn't going to give up. He called Russell stubborn, but Tris was just as bad in his own way.

Tristan pressed his lips together, but didn't speak until he'd pulled on a pair of black cargo pants and a soft black shirt. The color only made his brilliant eyes stand out more. "Do you care what I think?"

Russell raised his eyebrows. "Of course I do, but not if it means you're going to try and send me away." He noticed that Tristan hadn't bothered with socks or shoes. Somehow, that intimate little detail did what watching his lover completely nude in the shower hadn't, and his heart lurched as his cock twitched. *God help me,* he thought, knowing that no matter what happened, he'd always love this man.

Tristan pushed past him, heading for the kitchen. Russell trailed him, adjusting his erection. He knew now wasn't the time for more sex. They had to get in touch with Tristan's people and find out what the hell had happened in the aftermath of the memorial service.

Tristan opened the refrigerator and grabbed two bottles of mineral water, then turned and stared down at his hands as the appliance's door whooshed shut behind him. Russell was about to step forward, but then Tristan looked up, expression tortured. He carefully placed the water bottles onto the island. Instead of opening them, he gripped the back of one of the chairs and leaned forward. "They're going to come for me, Russell. You know this.

And I'd rather you live than spend your life protecting me. The cartel lost a lot of money when I shut everything down, and now that I know about their little side project with genetic manipulation, they're out for my blood."

Russell walked forward and gently pried Tristan's fingers free. "Tristan, you have to stop thinking in the short term." He kissed Tristan's knuckles and let him go.

Tristan frowned. "What are you talking about?"

Russell cracked open one of the bottles and drank half of it down in one swallow. Shifting always made him thirsty as hell. Shifting into dragon form seemed to amplify it. "You assume that they're going to come for you and kill you, and me along with you, but you don't have to wait. You can always take the battle to them." He leaned back against the island. "And I have no intention of dying anytime soon. I expect we will be alive for a long time together." He tilted his head. "What the hell did you think was going to happen when I came home?"

Tristan stared at him. "I ... don't know, actually." He ran a hand over his face. "I wasn't thinking. I was exhausted. I'm *still* exhausted."

Russell understood that. "You don't have to do it all alone anymore, Tristan," he said gently.

Tristan opened his bottle and drank. After swallowing, he sighed. "I'm sorry."

"I understand," Russell said, heart aching. "Of all the people in the world, Tris, I understand you."

Tristan smiled wryly. "I know."

"I think we should take your mother's ashes to the ocean today, instead of waiting," Russell said. He wandered to the refrigerator and opened it. Shifting also made him hungry. Thank God Tristan kept it well stocked. He pulled out sliced beef and cheese and lettuce, setting them on the island. Glancing around, he found a loaf of crusty bread. Five minutes later he had two sandwiches made. "I don't think we should let them regroup. If we can keep everyone guessing…" He trailed off and took a bite of his sandwich. After chewing and swallowing, he continued. "We have the advantage."

"We're outnumbered, though," Tristan pointed out, taking the plate Russell slid towards him. "It might work, or everything might go pear-shaped."

Russell shrugged again. "What the hell else are we going to do? Hide out in here forever?" He glanced around. "It's a nice place, but we can't spend the rest of our lives holed up in your tower." He grinned. "I'm no Prince Charming, and you're sure as hell not Rapunzel."

Tristan laughed. "I think you've got your fairy tales mixed up." He began eating. "You're the big bad wolf."

Russell smiled. "I don't really give a shit, as long as you don't morph into Little Red Riding Hood."

Tristan laughed, and then took another bite of his sandwich. They ate in companionable silence for a moment, but then Tristan sighed and pushed his empty plate away. "What *do* you give a shit about?" He held his face carefully blank.

Russell's smile fell away. Tristan couldn't hide from him, no matter how hard he tried, and he sensed his lover's worry loud and clear. "You. I give a shit about *you*, Tristan."

****

Russell's words hit Tristan like a punch in the chest. He *knew* how Russell felt about him. He'd known even way back when they were too young to be thinking about such things. They'd decided to swear a blood oath to each other, but somehow it never felt quite real until now. *Do the right thing, Tristan*, he told himself, but instead of speaking, he held out his hand, the one with the scar.

Russell clasped it, and their energy surged and mingled. "We make each other stronger."

"We make each other who we're meant to be," Tristan said, pulling him into an embrace. Russell's body felt solid against his. Tristan felt like he belonged in Russell's embrace. "You're hot," he said, instead of trying to put the complicated emotions swirling through him into words. He leaned back and smiled. He was still worried, but he'd deal with it. He slid a thumb over Russell's wrist. His lover's skin was near sizzling.

"So are you," Russell said, eyes crinkling at the corners.

Tristan rolled his eyes. "I mean, your body temperature. You feel feverish."

"It's the shifting." Russell shook his head. "It happened after I first changed shape into a dragon." He glanced at their empty plates. "And I burn a lot of energy, too."

Tristan nodded. "Makes sense."

"We need to find out if your people are okay," Russell said.

Tristan glanced outside. He didn't want to think about all of his responsibilities, but then he remembered the carnage at the service and grimaced, angry with himself. *You are not your father,* he told himself, knowing he owed his people his help, especially after the hell that they'd been through. "I'll get my phone."

Five minutes later, he dialed Meredith, hoping to God she was okay and had some answers for him. Russell said he'd seen Marlie go down, and Tristan knew the two women had gone to the memorial service together. Her phone rang precisely once, and then she picked up.

"Oh my God, Mr. Marik! Are you okay?" Meredith asked. "I couldn't find you, and then Marlie was hurt, and I—"

"Meredith, I'm fine." Tristan cut her off. She sounded frantic. "I was worried about you." He heard noise in the background. "Where are you? Is Marlie okay?" He frowned, worried about his assistant and receptionist. They might think he was a total bastard, but he knew better. He cared about the people who worked for him more than they realized, and Meredith had been with him for years.

"I'm fine, but Marlie was mauled by those monsters," she said, choking up. "It was awful."

"Are you at the hospital?" he asked her. She was usually unflappable, and hearing her voice shake felt like a punch in the gut. He should've protected his people better. He should've known better than to think the memorial service would be safe.

"Yes. Marlie is in surgery. They said she's going to be okay. Her leg had a bad laceration, but the bite didn't hit any major arteries. She was lucky." Meredith's voice calmed slightly. "Oh, her mom just got here. Thank God."

"Do you have a ride home?" Tristan asked her, worried that she was there alone. What if those bastards came for her? Or one of his other people? He couldn't protect every single one of Monolith's employees. He glanced at Russell, recognizing the worry on his lover's face. Maybe Russell was right about taking the fight to the cartel. He needed to stop this madness.

"One of your security guys came with me. Paul or Saul or something. Mr. Chesterfield assigned him to me for today. He can drive me home," she said, sounding distracted. "Marlie came with us this morning."

Tristan breathed a sigh of relief. He knew Paul, and he was a good guy. "Okay. Let him stay with you for today, and maybe tomorrow." He paused, thinking. He hated to ask her this, especially now, but he needed all the help he could get. "If you're feeling up to it, do you think you could do some investigating for us? See if anything has gone public? I'd really prefer to keep it all under wraps."

Meredith laughed, but she didn't sound amused. "Yeah, no kidding. There would be a panic. Fortunately, there was no media at the service, but the cops grilled me thoroughly. They don't want news of this getting out anymore than you do. The only reason I got away was because I needed to go with Marlie." She drew a shaky breath. "All the people who survived saw the wolves, but everything thinks it was some sort of hallucination. I know better." She stopped for a moment, then continued in a whisper. "And then there's the dragon."

"I understand," Tristan said tiredly. How the hell was he going to explain men shifting into wolves? Or Russell shifting into a dragon? Damn his father for developing the technology. Damn Russell's father for experimenting on his own child.

"Did Mr. Kelvin really turn into a dragon?" she asked tentatively. "I can't believe I'm actually asking you this. I feel as though I'm walking around in an alternate universe where the monsters are real." She sighed. "Maybe I need psychiatric drugs."

"Russell isn't a monster." Tristan fought down the surge of irritation her words spurred. He had neither the time nor the energy for anger, and she needed him to be calm. Even so, he knew he'd spoken too harshly from the look on Russell's face

"But the rest of them are?" Meredith's voice rose shrilly.

Wincing, Tristan looked at his lover. Russell grimaced, and Tristan realized he could hear every word Meredith said. "You're not losing your mind, Meredith,"

Tristan told her, working hard to be soothing. "It really happened, but that doesn't mean they're all monsters. Russell was born with the ability to change his form, but the others you saw were engineered. It makes them unstable." He was guessing at this, but when he caught Russell's gaze, he knew he'd hit the nail on the head. Russell was stable because he'd bonded with Tristan. The wolves had no such advantage. *Maybe we can use that,* Tristan thought.

"It was your father's research, wasn't it?" Meredith's voice had dropped to almost a whisper. "He was responsible for this. I saw references to it in the archives when you gave me access."

"My father didn't do the research directly, but yeah, he funded it and pushed for it. Russell's father was lead scientist on the project, years ago. He experimented on his own son because the natural ability runs through the maternal line. Russell had no choice in the matter." Tristan ran a hand through his hair. "I had no idea that the gene therapy was successful. Those wolves today were the first I've seen. I thought I'd managed to shut that line of research down years ago, but clearly some of it got out, and my father sold the technology, if not the actual research. It's worth billions, which is why he contracted with the cartel as a distributor," Tristan said grimly. He needed to tell her everything, but now was not the time. Hell, even he didn't know the extent of what his father had done. That was another thing he had to take care of.

"One step at a time," Russell murmured, correctly interpreting Tristan's roiling emotions.

Tristan gave him a tight smile. "Just sit tight this weekend, Meredith. If you can do some damage control with anyone in the company asking questions, I'd appreciate it, but not at the risk of your safety. The attack was part of a larger problem I'm in the middle of solving at the moment."

"What do you want me to tell them?" she asked him.

His gaze met Russell's. "Tell them the truth. Tell them that my father funded illegal experimental gene therapy and sold the results to the highest bidder. Tell them that I thought I'd shut it all down years ago, but that my father managed to sell some of the work without my knowledge. The FBI has all of the files, so the truth is already out there, somewhat. I gave them everything once my father was dead."

"Is that the whole truth?" she asked sharply, sounding a bit more like the competent woman he knew her to be.

"It is, actually. I've known about the experiments for years. I've been working against my father for years, trying to mitigate the damage he caused. It wasn't easy." Tristan hoped to God she believed him. He needed her help. *I hope she doesn't quit*, he thought, feeling the beginning of a tension headache stretch down the back of his neck. He rolled his shoulders, but it didn't help. He waited.

Meredith finally sighed. "I knew you seemed different this week, but I thought it was just the grief talking. Then, when you introduced me to Russell in your office, I didn't know what to believe. You treated him differently than anyone else. You seemed kinder, even with all of the stress of your father's death. I didn't understand what was going on." She made a sound in the back of her throat. "I'm still not entirely sure what's going on. What's the truth, Tristan?"

"I'll never lie to you," Tristan said softly, hoping she believed him. "And the truth is that my father has been a ruthless madman for decades, and I have a lot of work to do to dismantling his legacy. I may have to withhold information from you at times, but I'll never lie." With her help, deconstructing his father's evil empire and making sure of Monolith's success as a completely legitimate enterprise would be a thousand times easier. *She used my first name,* he thought, encouraged. She never called him Tristan. He hoped that meant she was considering what he'd said.

"Okay, I believe you, but we're going to have to have a serious conversation about Monolith," she finally said.

"We will," Tristan assured her. "I'll tell you everything I know. It may not be everything that happened, because even I don't know everything yet, but I'll tell you what I can, when I can. I'm still unraveling things."

She sighed. "I want to talk to Mr. Kelvin about what I saw, too."

Russell took the phone from Tristan and put it on speaker mode. "Meredith, I would be happy to answer any of your questions, but right now, Tristan and I have to deal with a very dangerous situation. What happened today was, well…" He trailed off before trying again, and Tristan knew he was trying to pick his words wisely. Neither of them wanted to endanger her with too much knowledge.

Not that I really know all that much myself, Tristan thought, frustrated all over again by his helplessness. He'd never expected an attack at the service. He'd never expected a pack of shifter wolves to show up, not when he thought his father's pet project with Michael Kelvin had failed years earlier. He could never have predicted that those men would go feral the way they had. He needed to do better.

"The truth is, we need to track down the men who

planned the attack and put a stop to them," Russell finally said. "I promise we'll explain everything when it's safe."

"I'll hold you to that," Meredith said, and Tristan knew she truly did understand everything they weren't saying. She'd always been intelligent. She'd had to be, to work for him and deal with his father without getting sucked down.

"Keep yourself safe, Meredith," Tristan said quietly. "I'll be in touch."

"Don't do anything stupid, Tristan," she replied, a familiar edge in her voice. "Without you running Monolith, I'm afraid of what might happen."

Tristan caught Russell watching him. What could he say that was the truth without horrifying her? "I'll do my best." He tapped the screen and ended the call.

"She's going to be a tremendous asset if we can keep her alive," Russell said.

Tristan snorted. "We need to keep *ourselves* alive, first."

"About that," Russell said, tapping a finger on the counter. "When we scatter your mother's ashes, what if we leaked our location?"

Tristan pursed his lips. "You mean, like bait?"

Russell nodded, gazing out the far window. "Exactly. If the cartel knows where we're going to be, and it's somewhere with less security than the formal memorial service, they won't be able to pass up the opportunity." He smiled, but his expression didn't look happy. "Hell, they weren't able to pass up the opportunity at the service, even *with* full security."

"I understand your reasoning," Tristan said, thinking it through. "Except there's only two of us, and God knows how many of them. It could be a slaughter." He rolled his shoulders, going over the situation in his head. "And even if we survive, there's no guarantee that the cartel won't just send more men after us. We need to cut off the head, not the fingers."

Russell turned to him, and Tristan almost stepped back at the look on his face. Russell looked both angry and resolute, and the combination was frightening. *And comforting, God help me,* Tristan thought.

"It might be a slaughter, but not because we're going to die," Russell said quietly. "I smelled an Alpha in the pack at the mausoleum. There's no way the cartel leader would be able to keep control of those wolves if he wasn't also a shifter. Wolves run in packs. Packs need a leader. And that technology is just too tempting for a criminal boss used to being in control."

"You think the boss man was there? At the service?" Tristan asked, surprised. "I didn't get even a whisper of him with my power, and I really should've picked up something. Hell, I don't even know his name."

"We don't need to know his name in order to kill him," Russell said. His voice was hard. "I am not going to spend the rest of my life looking back over my shoulder."

I don't want to watch my back for the rest of my life, either, Tristan thought. *That would be a grim existence.* He reached out and put a hand on Russell's arm. "Because you're not going to hold back."

Russell nodded, eyes dark and hot. "Because I'm not going to hold back. The beast will be who they'll face, not two vulnerable men."

Tristan let the thought of Russell's dragon sit in his mind for a long moment, and then he half smiled. "Let the beast have his day, and we'll see who's left standing at the end of it all."

Chapter Nine

The following morning, Russell watched Tristan contact Meredith and instruct her how and when to let certain business contacts know where they'd be later. He had a far more important thing to worry about: how long he could stay in dragon form before his consciousness disintegrated. When he'd flown Tristan home, it had only taken a few minutes, and he hadn't felt his mind slipping even a little bit, but he couldn't rely on that being the case the next time he shifted. That short flight was only one time versus over a decade of madness while in beast form behind him. If they truly had to confront an army of men bent on killing them, the battle would take longer than a few minutes, and there was no guarantee that he'd remain sentient. The thought of hurting Tristan unintentionally horrified him.

"Do you think you can do this?" Tristan asked him, as if he could read Russell's mind. He glanced at the small box on the coffee table. His mother's ashes nestled inside the innocuous container. Somehow, it seemed more appropriate than the fancy urn Tristan had used as a prop at the memorial service. Russell remembered Tristan's mother as a quiet, elegant woman. "Do you think *we* can do this?"

"I have to believe it, and so do you," Russell said, not willing to put his doubts into words. If he chewed on them too much, he'd make them true before they ever got to the beach. And, too, Tristan could sense what he was feeling. It was difficult to hide emotions from an empath. "You have to believe it. We have no other choice." He sprawled back on Tristan's comfortable leather sofa, pretending calm, when he was anything but. The inside of his skin itched. Deep inside, his beast paced the confines of his mind restlessly.

Tristan started pacing. "This is crazy. You *know* this is crazy."

"It's too late. We've already set it all up." Russell thought about how easy it had been to fall asleep next to Tristan the night before. What it had felt like to make love softly and slowly, and then drift off into the darkness. The sound of Tristan's breathing had soothed his beast, and that was when he'd realized he would do anything to keep Tristan alive, because he knew he'd been only half of a man for the past decade, and some of the time he hadn't even been that. Shifting let the beast out, and sometimes that was easier than living with the pain of separation, and he'd resorted to that kind of animal existence for far too long. He and Tristan needed each other.

And I will never go back to that half existence, he told himself. "Tristan, we have no choice. I'll destroy every last one of the men that try to kill you if I have to. I refuse to go back," he said aloud. "Even if it means my death."

Tristan stopped, looking startled. "You mean that. I can feel it." He rubbed his chest, as if the ache Russell felt had transferred to him.

And maybe it has. Tristan feels everything. That's why he's so wary of hope. Russell finally nodded. "Yes, I mean it. It was hell, living without you. It was hell, shifting and losing my mind and not knowing if I'd ever come back to myself. We knew better as teenagers. That's why we swore that oath to each other." He sat up, unable to maintain his pose of careless relaxation any longer. "I'm never leaving you again. If that means we both die, I'm willing to do that. Death is better than a life only half lived."

Tristan expression darkened. "I don't want you to die."

"And you think I want to die? Or that I want you to die?" Russell replied, angry now. "If you don't want that to happen, then you'd better be fucking motivated to stay alive, Tristan," Russell said, hands closing into fists. "Because I'm damn well not going to outlive you. If you die, I die."

Tristan stared at him, whole body vibrating. "I know you, Russell. You think you can sacrifice yourself for me. You think that you can die, if it means I'll live, but you have no idea that I feel exactly the same way you do," he said, sounding pissed.

Good, Russell thought. *If he's angry, he's not half asleep, trying to drift through life.*

"And fuck you if you think I'm going to just go on with my life if you die. Fuck you," Tristan stated, hard and angry. "If you die, I'm not going to spend one more minute alive than I absolutely have to."

Russell stared up at his lover. Tristan's eyes gleamed hot and angry, and Russell thought that he'd never looked more gorgeous. "Do you have her ashes ready?" he asked, instead of seizing Tristan by the arms and shaking the stubbornness out of him. He hadn't meant to ask that particular question—he knew exactly where the ashes were—but it slipped out, almost as an afterthought.

Tristan blinked at him, and then he exhaled, shoulders slumping down from the brittle posture he'd held too tightly all morning. "Yes. You know I do." He gestured to the small box. "She loved the ocean. She told me once that she wanted to get on a boat and sail away, and never come back, but my father had her watched almost twenty-four seven." He smiled bitterly. "She was never alone."

"She's free now," Russell told him, wishing that they were, too. All they had was hope, and he was holding onto it as tightly as he dared, but it felt like the tighter he gripped it, the more likely it would fly away. "We'll be free, too. Soon."

"Will we?" Tristan picked up the box. He turned it over in his hands, then slipped it into his pocket. "Seems like such a small container for such a vibrant woman." He looked up at Russell. "We should go."

Russell stood up. "Come here."

Tristan glared at him. "So you can rip my heart out? No, thank you."

Russell stepped over to his lover. "No. So I can give you mine to hold." He kissed Tristan, daring him to protest. They'd already made love, so why was it so difficult to hold onto each other? Why did it feel as if they were drifting away?

"You've only been home for two days, Russell. Try not to break my heart today," Tristan murmured against Russell's lips.

"I have no intention of dying," Russell said, trying to convince himself that he spoke the truth.

Tristan leaned back. "Are you ready?" he asked, instead of arguing, like Russell knew he wanted to.

Russell nodded. "Yes."

"Then let's do this."

****

Tristan let Russell drive the three hours to Shadmoor State Park. He'd wanted the time to think about what they were doing, and he wanted to watch Russell as his brain chewed through multiple scenarios of what might happen over and over again. Finally, he forced himself to stop overthinking things and just look at the scenery. His energy ranged out around them as the car moved, but he didn't sense anything out of the ordinary. Would he even sense anything? He'd been able to read people very well through the years, and influence them to a certain extent, but he hadn't been able to send out his power until Russell came home. He had no idea what he was doing.

"We're almost there," Russell said, taking the next right off the highway.

"At least it won't be crowded," Tristan murmured, looking towards the ocean. His mother had loved it here, on the few occasions that she'd managed to sneak them both away from his father for an afternoon. It was far from the city, and far from his father's fancy friends and snobbish business associates. His father had hated this place because it wasn't a private beach. There was never anyone to impress, here. There was just the wind and the low brush and sand. And the ocean, of course, with its unrelenting waves and deep strength. *No wonder he hated it. He hated anything bigger than he was,* Tristan mused.

"I haven't been here since before we swore our oath," Russell said, pulling into the parking lot.

Tristan tucked his mother's ashes into the pocket of his windbreaker. "It hasn't changed." He stepped out of the car. "I haven't been here in years, but it looks the same." His energy swept the area, but he sensed only a few other hikers. No one with any ill intent gathered around them. "I don't feel anyone nearby."

"We should hike to the beach, then," Russell said, locking Tristan's Land Rover. He pocketed the keys and joined Tristan. "The trailhead is that way." He gestured.

Tristan nodded and started walking. "What if our bait doesn't work?"

Russell kept moving. "Then we say a few words and scatter your mother's ashes. And we try again another day."

Tristan reached out and touched Russell's arm. "Thank you, for this."

Russell stopped, then took Tristan by the shoulders. "Your mother was kind to me when I had no one. I'm doing this for her, too." He kissed Tristan.

Tristan closed his eyes and let his power push through him and into Russell. When their energy collided, he shivered. Their synergy would never get old. "Let's do this," he murmured, breaking the kiss before he got carried away. They'd have time enough for messing around later.

Or at least, he hoped they would. *If everything doesn't go to shit*, he thought. The familiar sensation of events and people wanting to hurt him welled up, and he swallowed against the worry. Now was not the time to have second thoughts about their plan.

When they finally reached the bluffs, Russell paused, looking out over the ocean. "I want to fly out into that," he said, pointing to the sea. "It looks like freedom." He flexed his fingers. "My beast is itchy." He laughed, but he didn't sound happy.

Someday I want to hear a real laugh from him. And for a moment, Tristan wished he could shift, too, but then Russell turned to him, fire in his eyes, and the thought slipped away. He had enough already. He didn't need that power, too. He could already feel the energy of Russell's beast on his skin, wild and strong. "I'll hike down alone," he said, heading towards the trail that wound down through the cliffs. "You can keep watch from up here."

Russell grabbed him. "I'm not sure separating is a good idea." His worry crashed through Tristan in a wave, almost in sync with the real waves so far below. "If I lose you…" He trailed off.

Tristan squeezed Russell's wrist, then gently shook off his grip. "You can fly. I can't." He shrugged. "The more vulnerable I look, the more likely it is that the cartel will take the bait." He looked out over the beach again. "Life is all about risk."

"Life is also about being prudent. The fact that we're here without any backup is already a risk." Russell frowned. "All my instincts are screaming at me. Do you sense anyone around us?"

Tristan shook his head. "Nothing. Nothing except the ocean." The crashing waves below them drowned out anything his power could pick up. "The sea has so much energy it might be masking my abilities. I'm going down anyway." He looked at Russell, willing him to agree. "We have to do this. I don't want to spend the rest of our lives together looking over our shoulders every moment of every day."

Russell frowned, but then he nodded and stepped back. "I know."

Tristan wasted no time. He headed for the trail.

Twenty minutes later, he stood on the beach. The cliff hoodoos crouched above him like alien structures, while the ocean moved in front of him, blue and deep. He walked forward, drawing out his mother's ashes. When he stood at the edge of the surf, he opened the box. It wasn't expensive or fancy. His mother didn't need decoration, and his memory of her sure as hell didn't need it, either. He'd loved her, and for all of her faults and his father's machinations, she'd still managed to raise him with dignity and kindness. He held out the box, waiting for a good wave.

"Now you can stay here forever," he murmured, offering his mother's soul a mental kiss. "Thank you for being my mom." He crouched down and sifted the ashes into the sea. When the wind picked up, it lifted the last of them out of the box and blew them into the air, and Tristan couldn't help thinking that seemed appropriate, somehow. His mother hadn't been able to escape his father in life, but she could escape him in death. He sighed, casting out his power. The ocean still muffled his senses, and he stood up, hands crushing the simple box. Frustration welled up. There was no sign of anyone around. He could still feel Russell, of course, but their bond was stronger than the ocean. He looked up, squinting against the sunlight, but couldn't see his lover up on the cliffs.

"So much for bait," he muttered, pivoting to head back to the trail. The moment he moved into the shadow of one of the dunes that lay behind the beach, a pistol appeared as if out of thin air, and Tristan froze.

"All alone on the beach," the man holding the gun said, voice light. "Not very smart of you, Mr. Marik." His words held a hint of an accent.

Tristan looked into the man's lined face. Blue eyes stared back at him, hard and cold beneath a skull stubbled with grey hair. The man had the look of someone used to barking out commands and having them obeyed. Abruptly, Tristan's energy crashed through a barrier of some kind, and malevolence washed over him like a sticky fog. The old man had been blocking him, somehow, damn it to hell.

"Who are you?" he asked, even though he was fairly certain he already knew.

The leader of the cartel smiled. "Your worst nightmare."

Chapter Ten

Russell scanned the beach, but even his eyes couldn't see Tristan clearly from this distance. He cursed himself for not bringing a set of binoculars, although even those wouldn't help if Tristan had gone into the dunes. Alarm sizzled through their bond, and he knew *something* had happened.

"Dammit," he muttered, stripping off his clothes. He could shift while still wearing them, but they'd be ripped to shreds and he'd rather have a pair of pants to put back on if he had to let the beast out, not that he expected to end up back here if he had to shift into dragon form. He hadn't even brought his wallet or phone today, preferring to travel light, and now he regretted it. What if they needed to call for help? God forbid Tristan get hurt. He should've had some of Tristan's security people here as backup, and damn the consequences. He cursed again as he squinted, trying to find Tristan, but there was no trace of him near the surf.

"There's no help for it," he told himself finally, angry and frustrated and worried. Tristan needed him. He had to let the beast out. "And I thought coming home would be simple, idiot that I am." He ran a hand over his face. He felt like he was being pulled in a thousand different directions. He knew he needed height and distance to preserve the strategic advantage, but his heart told him he should be by Tristan's side. His instincts had been clawing at him for the past ten minutes, but he'd wanted to preserve his ability to think.

Too late for that, he told himself, finally shifting into a red-tailed hawk, a bird so common and ordinary in this area no one would think twice if they saw him. Though he was a little bigger than the usual size for the species, only a trained birder would suspect anything odd. His mind slowed down as the beast inside took over, and he railed against the loss of sentience, but then his consciousness rushed forward again, even as he launched himself into the air. Relief rushed through him as he worked to fly above the ridge.

Being so close to Tristan changes everything, thank fuck. Russell could only hope it had changed things enough. In the past, he lost his humanity far too quickly, and often far too abruptly to fight the process. Now, he sensed the beast coexisting with his human side, but he was afraid to trust that he'd retain the capacity for reason, so he had to work fast. He flew out and across the bluffs, catching a weak thermal to keep himself aloft as he hunted for Tristan. When he finally spotted his mate, shock pushed through him.

Tristan, he screamed, but his voice came out as a screech, and then his beast wrestled control away from him before he could do anything except register the fact that his lover was facing a madman with a gun. He screamed again, diving for the beach, talons out as if he could pluck the gun out of the man's hand, but even as part of his civilized side bled away, he retained enough sense to know that his options were limited. Men surrounded Tristan and the bastard with the weapon. Russell resisted the urge to rake his claws across the gunman's face, and instead landed on Tristan's shoulder. He wasn't sure why Tristan stood so still when there were enemies all around, but he supposed the cold metal of the gun kept his attention forward. The man holding it said something, but Russell could no longer understand language. He felt a rush of anger from Tristan, enough to make him mantle his wings.

When the sharp retort of a gunshot suddenly sounded in the space next to his head, he lost it. His beast shrieked, launching himself into the air before the man holding the gun could do a damn thing except stare at him in horror. He raked his claws across the man's face and the gun flew away, spattering more shots across the sand. Behind him, the scent of Tristan's blood dragged at Russell's senses, and he couldn't do anything except scream again and try to kill the pain welling up inside in a vast wave. He twisted, clawing the man again, hoping he hit something vital.

Somewhere behind him wolves howled and Russell shifted forms again, completely wild now as Tristan's pain burned along the bond. He was the beast. The beast was him. He could think, but he didn't need to when the only thing he wanted was destruction. His dragon roared flame down the length of the beach, igniting the wolves fast closing in on them. The man with the gun writhed on the ground, moaning, but Russell didn't give a fuck. He turned, half beast, half sentient, and found Tristan on the ground. Blood pooled from a hole in his chest. Surprisingly, his dragon receded somewhat, allowing the human side to slip back out. Russell didn't question it. He didn't care why he could control it. Tristan was dying right in front of him, and he'd do anything to prevent it. He shifted back into human flesh, gritting his teeth against the pain.

"Russell—" Tristan choked.

"Tristan." Russell fell to his knees next to his lover. "God. Don't try to speak." The gritty sand dug into his skin, but that small pain meant nothing compared to the huge, yawning terror in his head. The beast inside him lit his nerves with fire, and he had no idea how he'd shifted from dragon to human so easily, but he didn't have time to worry about it. He didn't feel entirely human, and he could see the residue of scales tattooed along his arms as he reached out for his lover. "Tristan, stay with me," he said, voice breaking. He put hands on

Tristan's chest, and the stark warmth of his lover's skin shocked him. Blood pumped out between his fingers, sticky and hot. How could it be so hot when he felt so cold inside? "Fuck."

"He was going to kill you," Tristan suddenly said, voice thick with pain. "I couldn't let—" He broke off, coughing.

Russell jammed his hands on Tristan's chest, pushing hard.

Tristan moaned.

"Shut up. Just shut the fuck up. Please." Russell looked around frantically, not sure what he'd find, but the charred bodies of the cartel's shifters were all he saw. No police, no ambulance. Tristan was going to fucking die here because they were too stupid and stubborn to ask for help. Why hadn't they told the FBI where they'd be? Why did they think they had to do this alone? "Tristan, no. Don't do this." He pushed harder. "You fucking fight for me, okay? Fight, goddamn it!" Russell glared at his lover.

"It's okay." Tristan shook his head weakly. "I'd rather die than let something happen to you. I'd do it again, Russell."

"No, Tristan—" Russell began, but then he heard a click by his ear and froze.

"You're both going to die anyway," a man said.

Tristan's eyes widened frantically, and he tried to push off Russell's hands.

Russell saw red. His anger and grief left his body in a mass of energy so unspeakably hot, fire blasted out around them like a bomb. The waves along the shoreline sizzled. The sand beneath them crackled. He couldn't see a damn thing, but he could feel Tristan under his hands, and his mind was utterly clear. He was going to destroy the men responsible for killing Tristan, and then he was going to let himself die along with his mate in a wall of flame. He heard shrieking, and almost choked on the scent of flesh burning, and then suddenly there was blessed silence. The red haze across his vision fractured, and he looked down as if in slow motion. Tristan lay beneath him, covered in blood, eyes closed. His face was so pale, Russell almost thought he'd missed the moment of his death.

"No," he whispered, rage welling up again, but then he felt something like a flutter of wings against his face. Tristan's spirit brushed against his soul, and he knew that this was it. His love, his mate, the man he'd spent half his life trying to come back home to...

Tristan was dead.

Russell flung his head back and yelled, enraged all over again, but Tristan's energy slid through him and into him, quieting his pain. He gasped, feeling as if half of his soul had been torn to pieces. "No," he said again, trying to grab at his lover with mental fingers. Tears wet his cheeks. "Don't go. Don't you fucking quit on me. Tristan, Jesus, fucking fight for me. I swear to God—"

"Russell, let go," Tristan murmured. His lips didn't move. His face remained pale and waxy, but Russell heard him loud and clear.

"Never." Russell shook his head and pressed hard on Tristan's chest, as if that could put all the blood back into him again. "I'm never going to let you go. Fuck that bullshit." He choked on a sob.

"Let me go."

Russell snarled. "No. Not in this life and not in the next, Tristan." In a quick, sharp motion, he slashed his wrists with his own talons, automatically shifting just part of his body. He didn't know where or how he'd figured out how to do that, and he didn't care. His blood poured out, thick and fast, like a red wave.

HIS BEAST RETURNS

That will do. That will do just fine, he thought, weirdly happy. Cold rushed in where there had been heat, and he felt his beast settle down as if for a long sleep. He would go with Tristan into death, then, and they'd be together. He put his head down and kissed Tristan one last time, and suddenly Tristan's body jerked. Russell almost backed away, but then he caught himself. He'd be damned if he'd let go now.

"Tristan," he said, feeling dizzy. God only knew how, but Tristan began to struggle, trying to get out from under his hands. Russell pressed harder, smearing their blood together. It mixed on his hands and Tristan's chest. He couldn't tell whose blood was whose, anymore. Tristan struggled harder.

"Oh no you don't," Russell said, throwing himself on top of Tristan. "If you go, I go." He no longer cared what part of him spoke. He didn't care if this was real or if they were both dead right now. Beast or human, dead or alive, it was all the same to him. He was the dragon. He was himself, and Tristan was his, and they would always be together.

"Russell, it *burns*," Tristan abruptly said, eyes suddenly wide. His pupils had expanded, pushing the green of his irises into a small ring. "Russell, stop it," he gasped, and then he blinked. When he opened his eyes again, flames danced in his pupils.

We must be dead, Russell thought, knowing that what he saw was impossible. "Tristan?" He could barely hold himself up. Shouldn't they be on their way? Why did he have to breathe? Their blood felt sticky and cool, and he didn't see any reason to try to hold on anymore, so he laid his head down on Tristan's chest. The flames in his lover's eyes soothed him. Tristan's emotions wound around his soul, and Russell felt love and peace, and then, out of nowhere, a rush of heat. His cock stirred, which was impossible. He didn't have enough blood left for *that,* and besides, they were *dead.*

"Russell." Tristan's voice shook his bones. "Russell, wake *up.*"

Russell shuddered, and then he gasped. He sat up. Tristan was holding onto his wrists. They were still covered in blood, but the wounds had closed. Russell stared at Tristan. His mate looked surprisingly alive, if a bit pale. In the distance, the ocean crashed upon the sand, constant and familiar, as if nothing had happened. Russell's heart gave a hard thump, and then another, before settling down into a steady rhythm. Inside his head, his beast circled, alert and … expectant?

"Russell." Tristan sounded impatient.

"Are we dead?" Russell asked his lover. Shouldn't they be dead? Floating somewhere dark or light or maybe somewhere in between? Somewhere warm. Instead, he felt very much alive, and sore, and … strange. He shivered. His knees hurt, of all things. He glanced down at his wrists, but the wounds had gone. Tristan's chest was healed and smooth, if a bit bloody. Russell reached out and swiped a hand over where he knew there had been a gunshot wound. Nothing. "What the fuck?"

He rubbed his wrists. Blood and sand ground into skin that was whole. Untorn. Meanwhile, Tristan's emotions scraped sharp as knives against his mind. His lover was relieved and angry and so very fucking grateful Russell felt his own eyes blur with the tears Tristan held back.

Tristan squeezed him on the shoulders, hard. Hard enough to hurt, and then he shook him. "We're alive." He inhaled shakily. "Russell, we're alive."

"Impossible." Russell shook his head, dropping his gaze to his wrists again. They didn't hurt. Hadn't he cut his wrists? "Everything about this is impossible, but I'm not sure I care." Tristan's relief pushed through him over their bond, and he tentatively allowed himself to open to it. To hope.

"Russell," Tristan said again. "I feel something that I don't understand."

Russell laughed, short and sharp. "I feel a *lot* of things I don't understand right now." He glanced around. There was no sign of any bodies. The faintest dusting of charred ash drifted across the sand, but the wind was quickly taking care of any evidence of what had happened. Beneath them, the sand crackled into sharp pieces, as if something incredibly hot had exploded right above the surface. *And maybe something had,* Russell thought, trying to reason his way through the confusion. He turned his hands until he could grip Tristan's forearms. "I feel your emotions. And my beast is calm. It makes no sense." He looked back up into Tristan's face. "We should be dead."

Tristan stared back. "Russell, there's something inside me. Something ... wild."

Russell frowned. Tristan's emotions twisted with his own, and all he felt was his beast sitting at the back of his consciousness, calm and ... happy? *What the fuck?* "Can you feel my beast, Tristan?"

Tristan nodded. "I could always feel you, but now it's stronger. Deeper."

"My mother used to tell me a story, before she died," Russell said slowly. "About her family, and how we held the secret of shapeshifting in our blood and our bodies. My father married her because he'd heard the story somewhere. When my mother discovered his research, she tried to leave, but the cancer killed her before she could go. She regretted marrying him. My father was an asshole. He wanted my blood for his stupid gene therapy experiments."

Tristan nodded. "We already knew that. You told me the about that when we first met."

"Yeah, but it was just a stupid story. No one had been able to shift for centuries. *I* didn't even believe it was real," Russell said, willing Tristan to understand. "It *wasn't* possible until I met you. Until we swore a blood oath to each other. That oath changed everything." He looked away. "I'm so sorry."

"Russell, I already knew that." Tristan's gaze felt heavy, and Russell knew his lover didn't want him to apologize. "I don't regret a damned thing."

"There's more to the story. More I didn't tell you." Russell took a deep breath. "Swearing an oath the way we did..." He shook his head. "I was selfish. I loved you. I wanted to keep you, so I talked you into a blood oath. I never believed it could be real." He made a sound deep in his throat. "I never expected your father to walk in on us. I didn't think he'd care. I didn't know I'd have to leave like that, and I've regretted it every single day since then." He grimaced. "And I should've come back a lot sooner. I should've helped you with him."

Tristan was already shaking his head. "No, you didn't coerce me into that oath. I wanted it. I wanted *you*." He frowned. "And my father was a bastard. A homophobic bastard. You being here wouldn't have changed anything."

"But I never told you the rest of the story," Russell said, reaching for Tristan. He had to touch him to make sure this was real. *To make sure we're not dead,* he thought, still feeling off balance. He wasn't sure he'd ever feel completely balanced again. Love did weird things to a man. "Tristan, I bound you to me, but only because I never really thought it would work. I thought the oath was all a huge joke. Just a family myth." He took a shaky breath. "The story goes that if two lovers swear a blood oath, they're bound for eternity. They share energy. They share power. And they share life and death." Guilt pricked at him, but he pushed it down. He couldn't afford to feel guilty, not anymore. Not when he *knew* he'd do it all over again. He'd swear an oath to Tristan a thousand times over if it meant they could be together. Love made him crazy, not that he hadn't realized it over a decade ago. "I thought it was just a story." He repeated himself. He couldn't seem to help it.

Tristan smiled. "But it's not just a story, is it? I've been different since that moment we cut our palms and held them together, all those years ago. Everything changed the moment our blood mingled." Tristan looked down at Russell's arms, and then at their hands, gripping each other as if letting go wasn't an option. "And now you've shared blood with me again."

"I did," Russell said, heart seizing as he remembered the lack of color in Tristan's face. "I wasn't thinking. You have to believe me. I just wanted to go with you, and if you were going to die, that's where I would be, too. I was okay with it." He inhaled, then let out the breath. "I am not leaving you again. You are not leaving me. I refuse."

"But I was dying." Tristan swallowed, hard. "I don't want you to die."

"If you had died, what would be the point of me living?" Russell felt the lump in his own throat. *This is what love feels like,* he thought, dimly wondering how it could hurt and feel so transcendent at the same time.

"What does your mother's story say if one of us follows the other into death?" Tristan asked carefully. "What happens then?"

Russell pressed his lips together. He should have known Tristan would see the point he was trying to dance around, mostly because he could barely believe the risk he'd taken had worked. "If one of a bound couple is mortally wounded, and the other shares blood with him, they can cheat death. It only works if they are fated mates. It only works if they share one soul between them."

Unexpectedly, Tristan smiled. "You idiot."

Russell blinked. Humor was *not* the reaction he'd expected.

"Russell, I already knew we were bound like that. I knew it all along." Tristan pulled him into a rough hug. "How could it be otherwise? I've known you are my other half since the day I met you."

Russell's eyes pricked. "You couldn't know. I never told you the rest of the myth. That's bothered me for years, but not as much as knowing I would do it all over again." He looked away. "I'm sorry. You should've had the choice."

"Don't apologize, Russell. Not for this. Not *now*." Tristan laughed. "Look at us! We're alive. I never in a million years expected to survive a gunshot wound like that. I *knew* I would die, and I was okay with it because it saved you. You deserved so much more after what my father did to you."

"What? No, that's ridiculous," Russell said. *He* wasn't the one Tristan's father hurt. "You're the one who had to put up with that bastard all these years. I was just off in the woods, doing my own thing."

Tristan snorted. "Yeah, off in the woods, alone, trying to remain sane. That was *so* easy for you."

Russell frowned. "I didn't have to try and keep my father from destroying people's lives. My father was already dead, thank God." He sighed, not sure how his apology got so off track. "I'm sorry I didn't tell you the rest of the myth. I'm sorry I didn't tell you the reality about bonding."

"It wouldn't have changed anything," Tristan said quietly. "I would still have done it. Hell, I would've done it *sooner.*"

Russell had no response to that. He felt exactly the same way.

"And I don't need a myth when I have the real thing," Tristan said, as if that were the most logical conclusion after everything that'd happened.

It wasn't. *It so very much wasn't. None of this is logical,* Russell thought, but he could see from Tristan's face that his lover was in no mood to listen to more apologies.

Tristan continued before Russell could argue with him. "The moment we swore that oath all those years ago, I began to feel different. My power to sense and influence people slowly emerged. You began to shift. Mingling our blood changed something in each of us, and I've never regretted it. Never." He shook his head when Russell tried to speak. "No, let me finish. I know it wouldn't have meant anything if we had been two normal people, and I won't lie and say that I understood that back then, but I figured it out after you left. So did you, or you wouldn't be here. There was something in my blood that made it work with you, Russell. We were meant to be together." Tristan shook him again, gently this time. "I *know* this. I've known this for years. I'm just sorry I didn't tell you sooner."

Russell stared at his mate, his best friend. His lover. "You're mine. Forever. You realize that?"

Tristan grinned. "It goes both ways, Russell."

Russell leaned his forehead against Tristan. "So it does." He sighed, not wanting to talk about reality, but they had no choice. He was standing on a public beach naked and covered in blood, and Tristan wasn't much better off. "What about the cartel?"

"They're gone," Tristan said simply. "The guy who shot me? He was the leader. I've met him before. He was a particular friend of my father. I hope they're happy in hell together."

Russell let out a sigh of relief. "No one else is going to come after us?"

"Twenty-odd men simply disappeared when they came after us. No one else from my father's world is going to come looking, because no one else is going to want to disappear. I'd say that's a pretty good incentive to leave us the hell alone," Tristan said, sardonically.

"We won't be able to explain it." Russell hoped they wouldn't have to. He looked out over the beach. A few clouds scudded across the horizon, and he scented rain on the air. They'd have to get moving soon. The beach was deserted right now, but only because they'd been lucky.

"No one is going to ask us to explain anything," Tristan assured him.

Russell, suddenly exhausted, decided to take him at his word. "I think it's time to go home, Tristan." He looked up at the cliffs, not looking forward to the hike. He'd have to shift into some other form—wolf, probably. He didn't think he could summon the energy that his dragon form required. A wolf would look enough like a dog to keep anyone who might see them from questioning Tristan.

Tristan pressed himself closer to Russell. "Screwing around on the beach while covered in blood is probably not a good idea, is it?" His warm breath tickled Russell's ear.

Russell shivered as his cock twitched. How in the hell was he feeling lust right now? "Probably not. Especially not when we're this exhausted." He looked down. "And covered in sand, as well as blood. Sand is abrasive as fuck."

Tristan sighed. "Maybe some other time. We've never messed around on a beach."

"I'm not slitting my wrists again just so you can recreate this bloody beach setting," Russel teased, but then his smile slipped away. "We haven't messed around in very many places." Theirs had been a long-distance relationship of epic proportions.

"We have a lot of places in our future," Tristan said, standing up. He reached out a hand. "I promise."

Russell stared at him, wondering how Tristan had managed to get to his feet after, well, everything. "I'm going to hold you do that," he said as he took his lover's hand. Tristan pulled him up, steady and strong.

Tristan's grip was firm and steady. "I'm looking forward to it."

Epilogue

"When you told me we were going to screw around in a lot of places, I didn't expect *this,*" Russell said, breath catching. Tristan had him pressed against the railing that overlooked the city on the roof of Monolith Tower. His lover bit into his shoulder, and Russell *knew* that Tristan was going to fuck him right here, where anyone could see. *Well, anyone with a set of binoculars,* he thought raggedly. This particular building towered over most of the others in this section of the city. He stared out over the side of the railing as if Tristan wasn't pushing his erection into his ass. He couldn't imagine how much hotter he'd feel if they were both nude, but he had a feeling he'd find out soon enough.

"You should have expected this," Tristan murmured, hands sliding under Russell's shirt. "You're the one who was staring at my groin all fucking morning." He ran his fingers over Russell's nipples, then drifted down. Russell's hips bucked as Tristan kept talking. "Even Meredith noticed your distraction."

"You wore tight jeans to the *office.* How the hell was I supposed to not look?" Russell asked incredulously. "You never wear jeans to work." He knew damn well that Meredith had been looking, too. *Everyone* had. Because while Tristan was a hell of a good-looking man in a suit, in casual clothes he was truly a sight to behold. *He'd* known that Tristan was fucking ripped, but he had a feeling that no one else had a clue until today. "Everyone was looking," he muttered, hands gripping the railing. In the back of his head, his beast growled. Lust had a way of bringing all of his baser instincts to the front of his psyche.

"I wanted to be comfortable." Tristan slid a hand down and cupped Russell's cock. "I wanted to be myself.

I spent over a decade pretending to be a carbon copy of my father. I buckled myself up in suits and ties, and I hated every second of it." He sighed as his fingers kneaded Russell's erection. "I'm *not* my father."

Russell shuddered. "That's for damned sure." His hips rolled into Tristan's perfect grip. He wasn't sure he cared anymore if anyone saw them. *You didn't care before,* he told himself, amused.

"Besides, you like it when I wear jeans," Tristan said, pushing his denim-clad erection into him again. "You like the look of my cock trapped behind the zipper."

"Jesus, Tris," Russell said, feeling every inch of that cock lodged up against him. "Fine. You've convinced me." He pulled away from his lover and stripped off his shirt. Unlike Tristan, he wore slacks and a button down. The buttons went flying. So did his shoes. Tristan grinned at him, gaze hot. "See something you like?" Russell asked, trailing his fingers over himself. He undid his pants and pushed them down, then kicked them away. His cock stood out from his body, and he gripped it, stroking himself slowly. When he reached down to cup his balls, Tristan groaned.

"Fuck." Tristan hurriedly pulled off his shirt and jeans. "You're going to kill me."

"Unlikely," Russell said, still stroking himself. "You're bonded to me, and shifters have a bit more stamina than the normal human, as you know."

"Whatever." Tristan stepped closer, then went to his knees. "Come here. I want to suck you."

Russell spared a brief thought of thanks that he rarely sunburned. It was high noon on a Thursday, three weeks after the travesty of the memorial service, and they were supposed to be in a meeting in a half hour with the FBI. Supposedly, the agency had news about a number of the ongoing investigations involving Tristan's father. Russell wasn't sure he cared, anymore. Tristan was looking up at him with those eyes of his, and his mouth, and—fuck. Russell didn't give a damn about anything except placing his cock on those perfect lips.

"Open up," he said through clenched teeth. He had to hold himself tightly at the base of his erection. Just the thought of Tristan on his knees in front of him brought him straight to the edge, and this wasn't a daydream. This was reality. Tristan's hair was mussed from undressing so quickly, and his green eyes glittered in the sunlight. His emotions rushed through their bond, and arousal, love, and a dash of mischief hit Russell square on, like a freight train. Russell bit his lip, imagining his cock sliding over Tristan's gorgeous lips. A drop of pre-cum slid from the slit, and he gritted his teeth.

"I didn't lock the door," Tristan said, moving closer. "I didn't let anyone know we would be busy." He leaned in and licked the tip. "Mmm. You always taste so damned good."

Russell groaned.

"You realize anyone could come up here," Tristan said, licking again.

Russell squeezed himself, hard. "That's bullshit," he gasped. "Only people we've put into the system can get up here." He struggled to hold onto the ability to think. His beast growled louder, and it was all he could do to keep from grabbing Tristan by the hair and fucking his mouth. He rubbed the tip of his erection along Tristan's lips. Stubble stung the sensitive skin. It felt good. Too good. Russell backed off a bit, but Tristan reached out and grabbed his ass, kneading the muscles. Russell shuddered.

"Meredith could come up here. Chesterfield could

find us like this. Me on my knees, and you about to blow," Tristan said, licking down the underside of Russell's cock. "Hell, anyone across the street could see us. We're not that much higher than that rooftop apartment across the way." He wrapped his lips around Russell and sucked.

Russell moaned. Tristan's mouth was hot and tight. "Stop talking," he said, gripping the rail behind him to keep from bucking. He'd given up squeezing his dick. It was a lost cause.

Tristan slid off with an obscene pop. "Your bare ass is on view to all of Manhattan," he said, slowly stroking himself.

Russell leaned over to watch for a moment, but then he closed his eyes as Tristan leaned forward again. If he had to look at his erection disappearing into Tristan's mouth, he wouldn't make it.

"Hmm," Tristan said.

The vibration of his throat against Russell's erection felt good, but it wasn't enough. "I thought you were going to suck me," Russell said, eyes still closed. He hung onto his self-control with all his will.

"I'm going to fuck you," Tristan said, standing up.

Russell's eyes flew open. Tristan smiled at him, bringing his hands up to show him a small packet of lube. Russell frowned. "Where did you—"

"In my pocket. I like to be prepared," Tristan said, ripping it open and smearing it over his erection.

Russell couldn't tear his gaze away. Tristan naked and aroused was one thing. Tristan naked, aroused, and smeared with lube was enough to make the beast within him growl with desperation. Russell swallowed again, but it didn't help. He felt dizzy. He felt like he was going to lose his mind if he didn't get to come soon. He took a shaky breath, but Tristan ruined every attempt at self-control.

"Turn around. Lean over," he said, stalking closer. His erection bobbed.

Russell licked his lips as his knees threatened to buckle, but he did as Tristan wanted. So what if he wanted to suck Tristan until they both lost their sanity? Tristan wanted him to turn around. Russell reached out and gripped the railing as he looked out over Manhattan. He was about to get fucked on the roof of one of the tallest buildings, in one of the biggest cities of the world, in broad daylight, and he didn't care one bit if anyone saw them. In fact, the thought of someone watching made him harder. "Hurry up," he gritted out of clenched teeth.

"Patience," Tristan said, stepping closer.

Russell could feel his mate's presence on his skin even before Tristan took hold of his hips. "I don't need patience," he bit out. "I need you."

"Good point," Tristan teased. "I'm not the least bit patient."

"That is completely untrue," Russell objected, thinking of the past decade. Tristan had the patience to deal with his father for all those years. He was the most patient person Russell had ever met.

Tristan chuckled, obviously sensing Russell's disbelief, but he also fit the head of his cock in between Russell's ass cheeks. "Fine. No prep. No taking our time." He pressed forward, gently. "I'm not going to be patient at all. I'm going to fuck you hard and fast."

"Jesus, Tristan. I don't need—" Russell exhaled as Tristan suddenly thrust up inside him. It hurt for a moment, but then his shifter power soothed the pain and his body opened up. Tristan groaned as his cock slipped right inside with no resistance. His thrust had been aimed perfectly, and Russell nearly sobbed as Tristan slammed right into his prostate. "Fuck."

"Yes. Exactly," Tristan said, voice ragged. "Fuck. Fucking you. I'm never going to get used to this. Every damned time it feels impossible." He pulled out and thrust in. "Astonishing."

Russell agreed. He tried to speak, but Tristan pulled out and rammed back in again. And again. Russell's cock banged against the glass railing. It hurt, sort of, and it also felt good. "God!"

"I know, I know. Hang on," Tristan said grimly. "I have no patience, remember?"

"Patience is overrated." Russell groaned, sliding a hand over his dick. It ached. He stroked himself. "I'm tired of patience. Fuck patience."

"Agreed," Tristan gasped as his hips moved, harder and harder.

"Yeah. Not like there's any finesse here," Russell managed to say. He liked when Tristan lost his veneer of civility. He liked the elemental desperation of it. His beast had stretched out inside his mind, and he knew his skin was heating up. He wouldn't shift in the middle of making love, but it'd be a close thing. When Tristan hissed, he knew his mate could feel the change in his skin. "Yeah. Fuck me just like that, Tristan. I can take it. I can take anything you give me."

Tristan fucked him harder and faster, head down on Russell's shoulder. Sweat coated them both. Heat had never felt so fucking good.

"This is insane. How can you take me in so easy?" Tristan asked. His fingers dug into Russell's hipbones.

"I can heal anything you do to me," Russell said, voice breaking on the last word as Tristan shoved inside him with a particularly vicious thrust. "Give it to me."

"I. Am," Tristan spoke through clenched teeth. "Take it."

Russell dropped his head down on his arms. He'd given up trying to fist himself in order to hold himself steady against Tristan's violent fucking. He panted with each thrust, and Tristan knew exactly what he was doing. Russell started to shiver, as if his skin had gone past hot and right into incendiary.

"Yeah, that's it. So close, Russell. So. Fucking. Close."

Russell bared his teeth as his orgasm abruptly crashed through him. His cock jerked, smearing jets of cum all over the glass without a hand touching him, which was crazy. He'd never felt anything like this before, even while in dragon form. Tears pricked at his eyes. Tristan knew him, inside and out. Tristan was inside him, climaxing too, now, and the heat increased. Russell didn't know how they kept from combusting, literally. He held onto the railing, shuddering as pleasure racked his body from his skin down to his bones.

"Tristan," he said, or maybe he only thought it, but his lover heard him and put his arms around him, and they slid to the flagstones, holding tightly to each other.

"I'm pretty sure Mrs. Montsurren has a telescope on her rooftop garden across the street," Tristan finally mumbled.

Russell started laughing. "Of course she does." He blearily eyed the streak of jizz decorating the railing. "And she probably saw the whole thing, because why not? Neither you nor I have any dignity left." He rolled over and dragged Tristan into his arms. He didn't give a damn about the lube or the drying semen or the sweat.

Tristan held him back, just as tightly.

"I love you," Russell whispered. He'd said it before, but he wasn't certain Tristan actually understood what he'd meant. *Although, the blood oath and the almost dying would have to be giant clues,* he thought.

"I love you, too," Tristan replied. "I know I don't say it often, but I don't usually jump in front of bullets for just anyone."

Russell grinned. "Yeah. I kind of figured that out."

Tristan sighed, relaxing into him. "The FBI will be waiting."

"Meredith can probably deal with them better than we could," Russell offered.

Tristan nodded. "Probably."

"That woman deserves a raise," Russell added.

"Already gave her one."

"Maybe give her another." Russell looked up into the sky. The cloudless blue was the perfect kind of flying weather. "We're going to be busy for the next few hours."

"Oh?" Tristan sat up, eyes gleaming.

"Grab your clothes," Russell said, already whispering to the beast in his soul. His skin prickled. He looked up, and Tristan stood in front of him. He had his jeans on, and he looked like everything Russell had ever wanted. He stood up slowly, nodding at the question on Tristan's face, and then he let the dragon out.

The End

www.erinmleaf.com

ERIN M. LEAF

EVERNIGHT PUBLISHING ®

www.evernightpublishing.com